THE ALIEN WHO WOKE EARTH

A FIRST CONTACT DRAMA

AIA PUBLISHING

REMI DEWITT

CHAPTER ONE

Devon was a princess. She knew she was a princess because her parents kept telling her so. Princesses were supposed to be loved, but now she knew her parents hated her. They must do because princesses were supposed to be beautiful and have beautiful things, but they'd given her something totally ugly, like completely horrible, disgusting, yuck. Today was her seventh birthday, and she'd told them what she wanted. She'd actually drawn pictures and stuff, and still they'd given her that *thing*. It was almost as if they were stupid or something.

They had to be punished, so she'd run away from her little party. Now she sat by their lake, staring at her reflection in its still water while the fingers of one hand ran through the long, brown hair tumbling over her shoulder. Her reflection stared back at her, but she wasn't terribly interested in looking at herself right now. Running away from her party wasn't enough. She wanted her parents to feel really, really sorry, like more sorry than they'd ever felt before.

She could run away some more. She could hide out in the woods for the night. Think how worried, and sorry, they'd be then. They'd come looking for her. They wouldn't find her, of course. She was much too smart for that. They'd call the police, and the police would organize a search with volunteers coming from everywhere. And the police and the volunteers would search and search, probably even sending a diver out into the lake. And then, just as the police and the volunteers were standing around not knowing what to do next and her parents were crying because they were so, so sorry, she would just wander along home and tell them how she'd fallen asleep inside a dead tree. She knew exactly which one it would be as well. Her parents would look really stupid then, right in front of all the policemen and the volunteers, and it would serve them right too.

She was—what was the word her parents kept using when they drove through poor neighborhoods with all the doors locked?—deprived. That was it. She was like all those other people who couldn't have what they wanted. It wasn't fair is what it was. It wasn't fair that all the people like her couldn't have what they wanted, and the reason for it was perfectly obvious. It was because other people, like her parents, didn't listen. All they did was make stupid rules that stopped all the people like her from having what they wanted, probably because they were stupid too.

God couldn't have wanted the world to be like that because God wasn't stupid. God was kind and loved everyone. No. It was the stupid people who did it, and for some reason, God couldn't stop them from being stupid. Perhaps God needed someone to do it for him, someone like Jesus; only Jesus didn't want to because last time he tried everyone had been nasty to him. Well, if Jesus didn't want to do it, maybe she could. She was a princess, after all, and princesses were supposed to make everyone be nice to each other; except she didn't know how to do any of that. God would have to show her, if that was what God wanted, of course.

Suddenly she heard a loud whoosh, followed by an even louder splash. Startled, Devon looked up and saw the middle of the lake boiling. Ripples spread outwards, then turned back on themselves, crissing and crossing until all the lake's surface was seething. The waves lapped at her glittery pumps, seeping in between her toes, even wetting the hem of her pink dress, but that wasn't why she stood up. No. She stood up because something actually, really magic started to happen. A head rose, followed by a body, all of it as seamlessly silvered as chrome. Though white where it mirrored the sky, deep greens and blues smeared its lower parts where it reflected the trees and the lake, and all the colors shifted constantly as it moved. It was almost like some knight from olden times, the kind that rescued princesses and made everyone live happily ever after. Dripping, it came to stand over her, but Devon wasn't afraid because she knew what it was. It was her very own gift from God because God did want her to.

So, with a smile, she introduced herself. "Hi. My name's Devon. What's yours?"

Its head gazed down at her, from a body so tall that it was taller even than Daddy, and he was quite tall enough. Well, Devon thought it was gazing down at her, anyway. It was hard to tell, what with its big silver egg of a head having no eyes or mouth, or nose, or anything at all, really. Somewhere inside that silver egg it must be able to see her, because otherwise it wouldn't be able to gaze down at her. Nor did it speak. Perhaps it couldn't, what with it having no mouth. Or perhaps it didn't understand. Everyone understood pointing, though, so she stretched out her arm.

"My home's over there. Well, it's not really my home. That's in San Francisco. This is where we come

4

on spring break so Mommy and Daddy can get away from the city. You should come with me because then they can see what the best gift in the whole world looks like."

She held out a hand for it to take, but it didn't seem to understand that either. This was difficult. She gazed at her reflection in its navel as she struggled with what to do. She couldn't very well make the world a nicer place—well, not easily, anyway—if this gift from God didn't understand talking or pointing or holding hands. Maybe it was a test. God liked to test people to find out if they were good or not. Well, that's what Mommy and Daddy said, anyway. He must have decided she was good, because all of a sudden this gift stretched out a hand and folded its three thick fingers with blunt ends over hers, swallowing them entirely within its fist. The faintest of pinpricks followed, making Devon gasp, but she quickly forgot about it because the strangest feeling crept over her. First her arm and then her whole body glowed with it.

"Ooh! I feel all warm and cozy inside. Can you feel it too?"

Probably it did because its hand was just as warm and not at all hard like a knight's armor would be. It was smooth and supple, almost like Jell-O wrapped in plastic, just squishy enough not to be yucky. Devon liked that too. It was making her feel super-happy inside, as if nothing bad could ever happen again, and she wanted more of it. The best way to do that was to make this gift her best friend.

When at last it released her hand and stood waiting for something, or so it seemed to her, she asked again, "So what is your name? Don't you have one? Oh well. I'll call you … let's see … I'll call you Auntie because I used to have an auntie who made me feel all warm and happy like you do. Her name was Rosita, but she went away. I don't know why. Now let's go see Mommy and Daddy. They're going to be really, really surprised when they meet you."

Up through sparse trees and tall grasses, she led the way. Auntie followed, her trail through the grasses indistinguishable from Devon's despite her hugeness. On the other side of a wide lawn stood the house. It had two stories with a veranda that sheltered the big downstairs windows and sliding doors. A person who stood beneath it could look out through the trees all the way down to the lake.

As they crossed the lawn, Mommy rushed out to meet them. Mommy was pretty. With her long dark hair and dark eyes, everyone always said how much she and Devon looked alike. She was even prettier when she smiled, but she wasn't smiling now. That must have something to do with the very big kitchen knife she held in her hand. At the very sight of it, Devon felt a chill creep over her.

Stopping some yards distant, Mommy gazed in horror at Auntie. "Oh my god, Devon. What is that?"

"This is Auntie. God gave her to me."

Mommy shook her head. "No, sweetie, that thing didn't come from God."

Daddy appeared. He was handsome, like a prince—square-jawed with tousled, light-brown hair. He was dressed like Mommy in casual pants and a loose shirt, but he carried a hunting rifle and leveled it at Auntie as he walked up next to Mommy. At the sight of that, the chill within Devon deepened so that she felt like ice cream inside.

"Mark!" Mommy sounded more scared than horrified now. "What do we do?"

"Just … don't do anything, okay? Stay calm and let me deal with it." Daddy sounded really brave, just like a prince ought to. "Devon. Princess. Come over here; there's a good girl."

Instead, Devon frowned. "Why? Auntie isn't hurting anyone. Auntie is going to make everyone be nice to each other."

"My god, Mark. What is that thing?"

"Christ, Sarah, how the hell do I know? Now just shut up and let me deal with it, okay? Devon, be a good girl. Do as Daddy says and just step away from that ... thing."

"But why? She's my gift from God. Don't you want me to have a gift from God? Why don't you want me to have something I actually like? Why are you always so mean? I hate you! I hate you! I hate you!"

As she howled her outrage, Devon's insides turned icy cold and two globules of brilliant red fire appeared from over her right shoulder. She had seen falling stars streak soundlessly across the night sky. Rather like them, these globules streaked now, one each enveloping Mommy and Daddy in a glowing red cocoon. Somewhere some angry cats hissed, or so it seemed to Devon, and when they were done, both Mommy and Daddy were gone.

Wide-eyed, Devon looked up at Auntie. "Did you do that? Where have they gone? Is it somewhere nice? It must be, mustn't it, or God wouldn't have let you do it. That must be right. God wanted you to do it because he loves them, and now they're with him, and he's going to make sure they're happy and have everything they want."

Auntie's only answer was the increasing warmth Devon felt. Despite that, she was still a little troubled. God was nice, and he loved everyone, or at least he did until they were bad. Mommy and Daddy weren't bad, not as far as she knew anyway, and he wouldn't have sent Auntie all the way here so she could do bad things. There must be another reason for making her parents disappear. It was hard to figure out what that reason might be. Then she realized that if God wanted her and Auntie to go out and make the world a nicer place, he wouldn't have wanted her parents telling her to go to her room or anything like that. He was just making sure she wouldn't have to worry about them when there was all the rest of the world to worry about, that was all. God really was clever like that, much cleverer than her, so she wouldn't worry about it, just like he wanted. Besides, right now there was something far more important that maybe God hadn't thought about.

"Do you know how to make dinner? Because I'm hungry."

Auntie didn't reply, not in any way at all. She simply stood there like a statue once again, as if she was waiting for something. It might be she was waiting to be told what to do, and it was up to Devon to tell her. That was probably right, what with God having given Auntie to her and not the other way around. It was just a pity God hadn't thought to show her how to make dinner was all.

"Oh well, never mind. Let's go into town. There are lots of places we can get dinner there."

Through the late afternoon forest, they walked.

Devon felt happy, eagerly pointing out things she thought were interesting or pretty so that Auntie might find them interesting or pretty too. There were all the big trees, and fallen trees, and the understory thick with ferns, and the singing of birds and all sorts of insects. All that was missing to make it quite wonderful was something magical, like a unicorn, and then suddenly there was one. It stood in the middle of a clearing, watching her. Really it was an elk. It was still adorably pretty, though, even if it did have too many wrong-shaped horns to be a unicorn. If Devon chose to think it was a unicorn, then it was, and nobody could say otherwise.

Slowly she walked toward it, wanting to pet it, and it didn't run away. It snuffled at her and allowed her to stroke its nose until its ears pricked. Then it disappeared into the trees. At the same time, Devon's insides chilled again. Somewhere above, she heard the *chop-chop-chop* of approaching helicopters. That was exciting. She wanted to watch the helicopters fly by overhead, but, for some reason, Auntie wouldn't let her. Instead, she led Devon to stand beneath the wide boughs of a tree. There they waited until they couldn't hear the helicopters anymore. Why Auntie should be so afraid of helicopters was a mystery. It must be something God had taught her.

By now, the shadows were lengthening. Devon

and Auntie walked on until sounds of men came to them from another clearing. At the same time, the *chop-chop-chop* sound of another helicopter drew near. While Auntie stood transfixed, her featureless face looking up through the trees as it passed overhead, Devon walked on into the clearing. Two men sat beyond a small fire, both of them dressed as hunters, with bows close to hand. They, too, looked up at where the helicopter had flown by.

"That's the second time today. What in the hell d'you think's got them so excited?"

The second man answered with a shrug.

Devon noticed they also had a truck. On the back of that truck, they had a dead and bloodied elk. These men had killed a unicorn, and they were laughing about it. That was horrible, so horrible that Devon could only stare at it—until one of them noticed her.

"What the …? Where did you come from, sweetie?" he asked. "You lost or something, wandering around out here in the woods all alone? Or are you a princess who's just escaped from an evil witch?"

He was trying to be nice, even if he did sound a bit creepy. At least he knew she was a princess. As for an evil witch, that was just silly. There were no evil witches around here that she knew of. There were some nasty unicorn killers, though, and that made her feel cold inside. "I'm not alone. Auntie is with me."

11

"Yeah?" The second man peered into the trees behind her. He wasn't nearly so nice. "Well, I don't see anyone. Your auntie must be a shy one. Hey, Auntie, why don't you come on out. We won't bite cha, I promise."

While Devon gave the second man an icy stare, the first leaned in toward him. "Hey, I know her. She's that rich kid from up by the lake. Her daddy owns some big tech company down there in Silicon Valley or something like that."

They exchanged a look, the kind of look grown-ups exchanged when they were thinking something kids weren't supposed to know about. Whatever it was, they began to look at Devon very differently, almost as if she were a unicorn, until their eyes grew wide and their faces filled with horror.

"Jesus Christ!"

"What in the name of—"

Silly unicorn killers! It wasn't Jesus who came to stand at Devon's shoulder. It was Auntie, and Devon watched as her red fire enveloped the men. Those angry cats hissed again, but they probably weren't half as mad as Jesus would be, if he got mad at all, of course, because he surely loved unicorns too, and these two men had done a very bad thing.

With the nasty unicorn killers gone, Devon looked at the poor dead elk again. She understood by now that when she felt all warm inside, it was because Auntie was happy. When she felt cold, it was because Auntie was unhappy, and when she felt really cold, Auntie made people disappear. If Auntie could do that, send people to God and all, maybe she could bring them back too. Maybe she could bring the poor dead elk back to life. As hard as Devon thought about it, though, Auntie did nothing, and the elk stayed dead. Oh well. It had been worth a try.

In the growing gloom, they walked on, with Devon feeling increasingly sleepy. Sometime later, she yawned, and Auntie carried her while she slept. When she woke, Auntie set her down, and they walked hand-in-hand together along a forest track.

Devon saw a big fire up ahead. At the furthest edge of its light, she saw the boughs of trees and the gables and broken windows of an abandoned lodge. There were people too, sitting and standing around it. From a distance, they didn't look like unicorn killers. They were far too noisy for that. Perhaps they were some kind of forest folk, like elves, who'd come out to play when no other people were around to see them. They looked like older boys and girls, four of them, dressed in jeans and jackets. Devon had never seen a real elf, so it might be they just looked like older boys and girls.

Either way, it was another moment of magic, what

with the firelight in the middle of all that darkness and the little people all around it. How strange that, until Auntie had come along, Devon had never known such wonders were real. Her parents must've known because they often went out at night, leaving her alone with a babysitter. Perhaps the unicorn killer had been right; she had been imprisoned by an evil witch. Not her parents, of course, but all those babysitters who just sat there watching TV all night.

Not that any of that mattered anymore. What did matter was that the people were having some kind of party, and a party ought to mean food. Since by now she was really, really hungry, she wanted to join them. First of all, though, she looked up at Auntie long and hard. Auntie probably didn't even know what a party was, and Devon was already beginning to feel the tiniest chill just looking at them. She didn't want Auntie to ruin it all by making these people disappear.

"Don't worry, Auntie. They're just having a party. You don't need to be unhappy at them."

The chilliness receded, and Devon's understanding grew. Auntie was listening to her. Auntie could be guided by her. Well, of course. God in all his cleverness had made Auntie like a puppy, and puppies needed to be trained or there would be horrible messes everywhere. Well, Devon would start training her right now. She would walk straight up to these people and make friends with them, and then Auntie would begin to understand.

At first, as she stepped into the firelight with Auntie at her shoulder, none of the boys and girls saw her. Perhaps it was the cans they were drinking from, or that strange pipe thing they were passing around that was giving off such a peculiar smell. As wonderful as all these things might be, what mattered to Devon was that she couldn't see any food. It was a strange kind of a party that didn't have food.

"Dude!" A skinny boy with shoulder-length blond hair was the first to see her. "Have I just lost a few months or something? It's not Halloween, little girl. No trick or treating for you."

Devon knew perfectly well it wasn't Halloween. It was a silly thing to say, but then this boy did have a very silly grin on his face. So did all the others, for that matter.

"Whoa!" The second boy had short, dark hair. "What's with the stormtrooper, bro?"

He sucked on the pipe and held his breath, which made him look even sillier.

"That's Auntie." Even though he didn't seem at all interested, Devon explained, "God gave her to me so I could make everyone be nice to each other."

"Shit, dude." Devon looked a little shocked. The

blond boy was surely old enough to know better than to use bad words like that. "You're gonna *make* everyone be nice to each other. What are you? Some kinda Nazi or something?"

"I don't know what a Nazi is. Are they nasty? Because they sound nasty."

"Well, yeah!" one of the girls said. She also had blond hair, but hers was tied up in a ponytail. "Nazis are, like, racists and homophobes and transphobes and all that kinda stuff. They just wanna stop everyone from being free to be themselves."

"Well. I can't be one of them, then, because I want everyone to be happy and have everything they want."

"Hell, yeah!" said the second girl. She had dusky skin and straight black hair. She also used bad words, but maybe that was just the way elves talked. "The sister's gonna build a better world with justice for all, except the Nazis, of course, and the patriarchy, and the haters, and the pro-lifers. My body, my choice, right? You can count me in, sweetie."

Devon didn't know what any of that meant. Since they were all so much older than her, she would trust they knew what they were talking about. She would remember that Nazis were bad people, and so were all the others: the racists, the homophobes, the transphobes, and the pro-lifers and such. These were the nice people. They would be her new friends, and friends helped each other.

"Do you have anything to eat? Because I'm really hungry."

"Aww, sweetie. Why didn't you say so? I think we might still have some pizza left. Come on. Why don't we go have a look?"

With her hand outstretched, the blonde girl started toward Devon. With every step she took, though, Devon felt the chill return. Auntie didn't understand friends either. Auntie thought this girl was going to do something mean. If Devon didn't stop her, Auntie would make this girl and all her friends disappear. She began to think very hard of nice things, like unicorns and fluffy bunnies, puppies, and popsicles. Gradually, the chill began to retreat. Auntie was obeying her. Just to be sure, Devon looked up at her big, shiny egg of a head glinting in the firelight. "Be nice, Auntie. From now on we only send Nazis to God because they're nasty. Not like my parents. That was an accident, probably."

"An accident." The blonde girl, standing a few steps distant, looked a little concerned. "What do you mean by an accident? What did ... Auntie ... do to your parents?"

"Oh, she made them disappear. She didn't mean to. She didn't understand, is all, but I'm teaching her. From now on, she'll only make the bad people disappear. Like the unicorn killers."

That only made things worse.

"The unicorn killers?" The girl backed away, saying to the blond boy, "We gotta get outta here."

"Get outta here?" he sniggered, too wrapped up in his silliness to notice her unease. "Why? We still got beer and, like, a whole bag of weed. Chill out, babe. We got all night."

"Listen to me, will you? That thing—if I'm hearing her right, that thing kills people. We gotta leave now!"

The boy with the short, brown hair wasn't listening either. "Of course it does, babe. It's a stormtrooper. That's, like, what they do. Look out! It's reaching for its blaster."

The dark-haired girl laughed too, but Devon could see the blonde girl was being very serious. She didn't like Auntie at all. In fact, she was afraid of Auntie. That wasn't good because she'd been the only one among them who'd actually listened to Devon, and the only one who'd offered to find Devon something to eat—until she got scared. It was time to leave before Auntie got scared too.

"Oh well. We're going into town now. I hope you enjoy the rest of your party. Bye."

CHAPTER TWO

Auntie carried Devon through the darkened trees. As they went, Devon tried to train her some more. "You're only allowed to make things disappear when I say so, okay? Like, that tree, and that tree, but not that one."

Balls of light flew and the first two trees disappeared, but the third one remained unharmed. The angry cats hissed as if they followed Auntie around just waiting for her to make things disappear, but this time Devon hardly noticed. She was too busy making sure Auntie understood.

"You see? It's easy. Make things disappear when I say so, and only when I say so, or I might have to get mad at you."

Auntie walked on, neither hot nor cold. If the lesson had been learned, she wasn't telling.

Sometime later, they came to a road that ran alongside a large body of water. Auntie stepped onto the road and carried Devon around a slight curve with buildings to their left and right. They entered a town, the first one they'd come to. Devon felt pleased because she'd surely be able to find something to eat here.

Before they could find a store or something, they came upon a junction with another road that swung in from the left. Street lights on either side of it cast bright pools of light onto the pavement beneath. Just before the second pool, lights mounted on top of a big, black vehicle flashed. They made Auntie unhappy, so unhappy that, without being asked, she set Devon down. As they walked on side by side, passing a sign that said they were heading into a place called Belfair, Devon looked up at her. "Be good, okay? Don't make anyone disappear unless I tell you to."

Auntie's chill remained. It didn't get any worse, but still, something was making her unhappy. That vehicle with the flashing lights had to be a police car, unless Auntie could see something Devon couldn't. That was possible, what with her being able to see anything at all with no eyes. It could be that vehicle wasn't a police car, then; it was only pretending to be. It might actually be some horrible monster that came out at night to scare people with its big, flashing eyes and then carry them away to its lair where it would eat them all up, and they would never be seen again. Not until they were close enough for Devon to be able to read the writing on the side of it did she smile.

"See, scaredy-cat. It's only the sheriff. You don't have to be afraid of them."

Just beyond the sheriff's vehicle stood a truck. The blonde girl from the party stood between them. She'd been nice to Devon until she'd gotten scared. She didn't seem at all scared now. In fact, she was really mad, probably because the sheriff, or one of his deputies, had pulled her over. With one hand held up and the other clutching a notebook, he was trying to talk to her, but she wasn't listening. She was shouting at him, waving her hands in the air and occasionally pointing in the direction Auntie and Devon had come from.

When they came within fifty feet or so, at last, he saw them. His hand froze in midair and his jaw dropped. Following his stare, for an instant, the girl froze too, until she thrust a pointing finger at them. "See! Do you believe me now, deputy? That's them, just like I've been telling you."

The deputy continued to stare, awestruck. Devon was pleased. People should think Auntie was as wonderful as she did.

With the deputy all but ignoring her, the blonde

girl wasn't pleased at all. She even went so far as to give him a little shove. "Well? You're the law, aren't you? For Chrissakes, do something!"

He still did nothing, so the girl pushed him again. "Hey. Wake up. That thing is dangerous. You need to call some backup or something."

Devon gasped at how brave she was. Pushing an officer of the law was a very bad thing to do. It was called assault or something like that. When the deputy woke out of his trance, for sure he'd be mad at her for it and maybe take her away to where all the bad people went. Instead, he put away his notebook, threw back his shoulders, and very slowly and deliberately came forward. When close, he leaned down to talk to Devon eye to eye, trying to be nice but stern at the same time. "Hey, little girl. So this is your Auntie, right? Could you ask her to take off her helmet so I can see her face?"

"Oh, I don't know if she can. She might not even have a face."

He didn't like that, not one little bit. With his hand moving toward his firearm, he turned his attention to Auntie, now all sternness and not nice at all. "I'm sorry, ma'am, but I'm gonna have to insist. Take that helmet off. Now!"

Auntie stood motionless, a towering silence at least a head taller than the deputy, her skin contoured silver and black in the street lights. With her chillness unchanged, she must be waiting for Devon to tell her what to do, except Devon didn't quite know. If that sheriff's vehicle had been some horrible monster, then this deputy would have been its servant, like some evil knight who went around everywhere being nasty to everyone. Then she remembered what the blonde girl had told her. This deputy wasn't an evil knight at all. He was almost certainly something else.

"Are you a Nazi?"

Now he began to look like an evil knight, his face clouding over with a dark scowl. "A Nazi! What the hell, kid? I'm a deputy with the sheriff's department. Now tell your auntie to take off that helmet."

"I don't think she wants to, and you wouldn't be telling her what to do unless you were a Nazi."

"Okay. I'm getting tired of this. If you don't take that helmet off, I'm gonna have to arrest you. Then I'll have to call child services, and they'll come and take the kid away. Is that what you want?"

Devon understood that. This Nazi wanted to take her away. Now she knew exactly what to do, and she pointed at him so Auntie would know exactly what to do as well.

"Auntie. Fire."

Auntie pointed too. From the blunt tip of her finger, a red ball flew. The angry cats hissed and the deputy disappeared.

"That too."

From another finger a blue ball flew, and the sheriff's vehicle folded in on itself, crunching and grinding and squealing until it had entirely disappeared into nothingness.

The blonde girl clasped her hands to her mouth. Horrified, she turned, probably meaning to run for her truck. Before she could, another red ball flew and, hissing, she disappeared. Then another blue ball flew and her truck crunched and squealed into nothingness too. Devon wasn't pleased. The deputy probably had been a Nazi, so that was okay. Even if she was wrong, God would sort it all out. The girl had been nice, though. She'd offered to find Devon something to eat while all the others around the big fire just sat there being silly.

Turning on Auntie, Devon showed her how mad she was by giving her a very big slap on her great silver leg. "No! What did I tell you? You're only allowed to make people disappear when I say so. Don't do it again or … or … I'll be so mad you won't like it one little bit!"

Auntie simply stood, her only reaction the warming Devon felt flow through her. She might not even be listening, except of course she must have been when Devon told her to fire. Then she wouldn't stop, which was willful disobedience. She ought to be sent to her room with no dinner for that, only there was no room to send her to, and thinking of dinner only reminded Devon of how hungry she was.

"Oh well. I forgive you this time, but only this time. Now come on. Let's go find a store or something. There must be one that's open. There always is back home."

They walked on, following the road for some distance, passing single-story buildings separated by stands of trees until they came to a red barn with lots of cars parked outside and people coming and going. More importantly, a sign promised lunch and dinner, which was exactly what Devon was looking for.

There was just one problem. "Do you have any money? Because we have to pay for things down here."

Auntie's great, silver egg of a head gazed blankly forward, leaving Devon to figure out what a silly question that was. Of course Auntie didn't have any money. Everything was free in Heaven. Everything would be free down here too, if it wasn't for those people who stopped everyone else from having what they wanted. Everyone should stop using money. It was as simple as that. Then everyone could have everything they wanted, and no one would have to go without. That must be what God wanted too;

otherwise, he would've given Auntie some money. Not that any of that was any help right now. If she was going to get something to eat, she would have to find some money to pay for it. Well, there must be some nice people here who would give her some money because that's what nice people did when others were in need.

"You wait here, okay, and don't make anyone disappear unless I tell you to."

Auntie obeyed, and Devon went into the parking lot alone. An elderly couple who were just about to leave looked like nice people, so boldly she walked up to them. "Hello. My name's Devon. Will you give me some money because I'm hungry?"

"Why, hello, sweetie." The lady smiled down at her like Gramma used to before she went to be with God. "What are you doing out at this hour all on your own?"

"Oh, I'm not on my own. I'm with Auntie, but she doesn't know what money is. I don't think she knows what being hungry is either, what with her not having a mouth and all."

"Really?" The lady's smile faded somewhat. "Well, that's very strange, isn't it? So where's your Auntie right now?"

Devon pointed, but the man had already looked. Not at all happy with what he saw, he'd already opened the driver's side door. "Get in the car, Laurel. We're leaving."

"But Pat, we can't just leave her here. She's a child, out here at this time of night. Where are her parents, and who is this Auntie who has no mouth?"

"Someone you don't want to meet. Now get in the car, Laurel. We're leaving!"

"Why, Patrick William Devers!" Laurel sounded just like Mommy had when there was an argument to be won. "All these years of marriage, and I never knew you could be so hard-hearted. Really! Shame on you!"

Pat shook his head, just like Daddy had when he saw that face and knew he was going to lose. "Well, fine. Put her in the back, then. We'll take her down to the sheriff's department."

And just like Mommy, Laurel smiled again. "There. Now you can come with us, and we'll take you somewhere safe."

She reached out to touch Devon's shoulder, and Devon instantly felt the plunging chill of Auntie's unhappiness sweep through her. It was far too strong for even an army of fluffy bunnies to stop, so she gazed up at Laurel with one of her most serious looks. "You better go now. Auntie thinks you're a Nazi."

"Laurel!" Pat was watching as Auntie advanced upon them. "Get in the damn car, for Chrissakes.

We're leaving! Now!"

Laurel straightened. Her smile wilted as, finally, she saw Auntie too. "Oh my. Oh dear lord. Quickly, Pat. Start the car."

Nor was it just Laurel and Pat. By now, other people had noticed Auntie and they became just as flustered. Some fumbled about as they tried to get into their cars. Others ran away or disappeared back into the restaurant. That made other people come out of the restaurant. When they saw Auntie, they became flustered too. In fact, everyone got into a panic. Auntie scared all of them and they, in turn, scared Auntie. Her chill became colder and colder. At any moment, she might start making people disappear, and that wouldn't be good at all.

Devon thought of nice things again, of puppies and ponies and mugs of hot soup clasped in mittens on a white winter's day. She wrinkled up her brow and thought really hard, harder than she'd ever thought before, and at last, it worked. Slowly the chill lessened. Auntie's determined stride did too until she came to a halt. Everyone else stood around as if frozen, or as if they'd also been calmed by all of those puppies and ponies and mugs of soup. More importantly, now they'd all calmed down, she might be able to get something to eat as well, which was all she wanted in the first place. There had to be someone here who would give her some money so that she could pay for it.

Before she could ask, the night echoed with the sound of approaching sirens. Two vehicles came howling into sight, screeching to a halt some yards distant. Out of each of them leaped another Nazi, both of them with firearms in hand. That wasn't right at all. Nice people ought to be able to go out at night without being afraid Nazis were suddenly going to turn up and start telling them what to do. Pat and Laurel had already driven away, but all these other people needed someone to protect them. How lucky they were that she and Auntie had shown up at just the right time.

Devon stopped thinking about puppies and ponies. The time for nice thoughts was over. These Nazis had to be stopped, and she did not hesitate to point at them.

"Auntie. Fire."

Two red balls flew. Both Nazis glowed for an instant, then disappeared. Even as the hissing cats fell silent, two blue balls followed, and both their howling vehicles loudly crunched and crumpled into nothingness as well. Everyone had been saved, which was good, only now Auntie was free, which was not so good. With her arm still outstretched, she meant to start making all these other people disappear as well.

"Auntie! No!" Just as mad as she could be, Devon marched up to confront her. "Stop being so mean! I really, really mean it. If you don't start behaving, I will punish you."

Auntie stopped. Her arm was still outstretched and her coldness remained, but at least she stopped. Devon sighed. For some reason, God had made Auntie really difficult to control. It was almost as if he wanted her to make everyone disappear, but that couldn't be right. The world wouldn't be a nicer place if there was no one left in it. It would just be empty. It must be another test then. God wanted to be absolutely sure that Devon was good. She'd heard grown-ups say that God never sent anyone a test he knew they couldn't handle. She'd never understood that. It sounded an awful lot like the teacher asking everyone in class to make something nice and then giving everyone a prize no matter how horrible what they'd made was.

Oh well. God must know what he was doing, and Devon still had to deal with Auntie. "Just be nice, okay? Not everyone's a Nazi, so stop trying to make everyone disappear."

Auntie warmed again and her threatening arm dropped to her side. There. A little scolding and a little love; that was all it took. Promising herself to remember that, Devon turned to face the people in front of the restaurant. They all looked like scared little bunnies that didn't quite know whether to keep running or stay where they were. One of them wore an apron, the kind servers wore, with the little pockets for pens and an order pad. Good, because the rumbling in Devon's tummy was louder than it had ever, ever been.

"I want a burger, please. And fries. And some ice cream. And one of those really big sodas. I don't mind which kind. Go get them for me."

The woman returned her gaze. Like all the rest of them, she didn't quite know what to do. Devon waited patiently, but with her arms folded and a very determined look on her face.

The woman glanced at Auntie and then back to Devon. That was enough to make her take out her order pad. "A burger with fries, ice cream, and a soda. Anything else?"

"I'm only seven. I can't eat everything, even if it is my birthday."

"Oh. Well, happy birthday, I guess. Would you like some party hats with that?"

Devon shook her head. She had already had a party, and there were far more important things than party hats to think about. Everyone was afraid of Auntie, but then, of course they would be. Jesus would've told God that people didn't always do what they ought to. Sometimes they had to be scared into it. Perhaps God should've given Jesus an Auntie of his own. Think of all the bad things that might not have happened if he had, not least to Jesus himself. Now God was trying again because he was really patient like that. It hadn't been enough that he'd flooded the world, with only Noah and everything in the Ark being saved, or those two towns he'd destroyed because they were full of bad people. This time he'd chosen Devon to help him, and given her Auntie to take care of all the Nazis—if she could only be properly trained.

The woman returned with a takeout bag in one hand and a large cup in the other. This time she was smiling, like grown-ups did when they were trying too hard. "Here you go, sweetie: burger, fries, ice cream, and a soda."

As she took them, Devon remembered. "I don't have any money to—"

"Oh, that's okay. It's your birthday. We want you to have them on us, so enjoy."

"Thank you."

The woman, and everyone else, continued to stand as if they meant to watch Devon eating. That wasn't very nice. She wasn't a monkey in a zoo, after all. "Okay. You can all go now."

Car doors slammed and grit flew beneath spinning wheels. When all was quiet again, Devon turned to Auntie. "I think we better go too. Perhaps we ought to walk through the trees, just in case any more Nazis turn up. I think we've sent enough of them to God for one day, and you can carry me while I eat."

Across the road and into the trees, they walked, leaving the town behind. Somehow, Auntie could easily see her way through the darkness and, safe and snug in her arms, Devon ate her meal, following each mouthful of succulent burger with a scoop of vanilla coldness—just because she wanted to, and there were no grown-ups there to tell her she couldn't. At the same time, she thought about all the things she hadn't asked Auntie yet. "So what's God like?"

Hardly noticing the lack of a reply, she went on, "I bet he's really nice and, of course, he likes kids most of all because that's what Jesus said. Does he hold parties for all the children and give them nice presents when it's their birthday? Does anyone even have birthdays in Heaven, what with it being forever and all? They must do because children can't stay children forever, can they? That wouldn't be any fun at all. Imagine having to do what your parents told you forever and ever. No. Children must grow up, so they must have birthdays, mustn't they? What kind of presents does God give them, then? Do they get puppies and ponies, or aren't they allowed? I wanted a puppy, but my parents wouldn't allow it.

"Oh, but do they even have animals in Heaven and, if they do, who looks after them? Do the angels look after them, or do they have other things to do? But then, of course, they're angels so they must have lots of things to do, like making sure Heaven works properly, or answering all those prayers, or coming down here and telling people not to be mean. So who does look after all the animals, then? Are the people who look after them the ones who looked after animals when they were down here? Do policemen and teachers have to be policemen and teachers in Heaven as well? Or does everyone get to be whatever they want to be?"

Devon gasped. "Could I be a boy in Heaven, if I wanted to be? I don't want to be a boy because boys are mean, but if I wanted to, could I? And, if so, could a boy be a girl if he wanted to? But that wouldn't work, would it? Boys are so noisy and always getting into trouble and breaking things. I know there are boys who want to dress like girls because they keep coming to our school and telling us about it. They're not very good at it, though, what with all that horrible makeup that makes them look like witches. It would be nice, though, if boys did become girls, because then we could all play at being family. But if all the boys became girls, who would play at being daddy? I guess someone would have to pretend, or maybe not all the boys would be allowed to become girls. That would be unfair, though, wouldn't it? And who would decide, anyway? I suppose God would, but then didn't God already decide when he made us all boys and girls to begin with?

"Oh, I don't know. It's all very hard. I'm glad I'm not God. Don't be sad, Auntie. That doesn't mean I'm sorry God gave you to me. God wants me to help him make the world a nicer place, and I will. I just wish it was a bit easier, is all. Oh well, I'm sleepy now. Be good, Auntie, and wake me up when it's time for breakfast."

CHAPTER THREE

Devon woke, warm and cozy in Auntie's arms. Like her hands, her arms had a gently giving surface, so Devon might've been lying on firm cushions with Auntie's shoulder as her pillow. The sun was barely above the horizon, and she felt happy to lie still while Auntie carried her through trees a little to the right of a highway. Where they were exactly, she didn't know. Where they were going, she hadn't thought about yet. They had to be going somewhere or they might just as well have stayed in the house by the lake. She would probably have to make her mind up about it soon. For now, she was happy to let Auntie take her wherever she was going. It would be an adventure, like a girl going off to discover that she really had been kidnapped by gypsies, and she really was a princess after all.

Auntie stepped out of the trees onto part of the road separated from the traffic by large concrete blocks. Up ahead, Devon saw the tall towers of a big bridge. Auntie took her toward this, passing by a long, low building on their right. At this time in the morning, hardly anyone was about to see them. The few cars that passed by on the highway didn't seem to notice them. Perhaps she and Auntie had become magically invisible because God didn't want anyone to see them yet. Well, that was one way to stop Auntie from making all the wrong people disappear.

On they went: around a shallow curve, between short concrete walls, and onto the bridge. Over the parapet to their right, Devon looked down upon a wide expanse of water, its opposite bank sitting low upon the horizon. Now the cars that drove by slowed a little, and some of the drivers craned their necks to look. God couldn't have made them invisible, after all. As if to prove it, a pair of approaching cyclists slowed to a stop some yards distant, and Devon felt the warmth begin to drain from her.

"Auntie. Be nice."

Auntie stopped, steadying into coolness as she waited for Devon to decide what to do. Devon wasn't even thinking about it. She was thinking about what a pity it was God hadn't made them invisible. It would be quite funny to be able to walk around without anyone knowing they were there and even funnier to be able to say something to them and watch them jump because there was no one there. Oh well. God probably thought they had more important things to do than play silly jokes on people.

The cyclists certainly seemed to have more important things to do. After a few moments of staring wide-eyed, they turned their bikes around and headed back across the bridge, their legs pumping the pedals as fast as they could go while they looked back to see if they were being followed. That was probably a good thing. No one had accidentally disappeared, and God didn't have another mess to deal with. Devon was happy. Since she was happy, Auntie was happy too.

On the far side of the bridge, the concrete blocks continued on their left while trees and the roofs of houses appeared on their right. A sign said Welcome to Tacoma.

Not far beyond, the concrete blocks ended at a junction. Too late, Devon realized another thing Auntie didn't know about—how to cross a highway safely. God mustn't have told her about always crossing in the proper place and always looking both ways first. She carried Devon right out into the middle of the road, and a car screeched to a halt just a few feet from them. Devon could see the driver clearly. At first, he was very angry. He began to open his mouth—probably to bawl them out—then he had second thoughts, his eyes widening like the cyclists'. As quickly as it had come, the car screeched backward, slewed around, and raced away along another road.

Auntie didn't even notice. She just continued on, following a rising path that ran between trees to their right and lawns separated by flower beds to their left. There were stone slabs too with lots of names written on them, and a flagpole. At the top of the path, beyond a long stretch of lawn, was a parking lot, and then a wide street lined with stores and vacant lots. A few blocks up, a big sign said Breakfast, and Devon decided it was time to eat.

After crossing the road, they walked through the parking lot to the drive-thru window. Two cars waited in front of them. The first one took its order and left. The second one must've decided it wasn't hungry after all; it sped away after the first without even stopping to order.

On the other side of the window sat a girl about the same age as the boys and girls around the fire. At first sight, she didn't seem as silly as they'd been, but that didn't stop her from not noticing her new customers as she cheerfully continued talking with someone Devon couldn't see. She mustn't have heard them because they didn't have a car. That meant she wasn't paying attention to her work. Daddy would've gotten very annoyed about that. People not doing what they were paid to do always made him mad. Devon usually felt rather sorry for them, until now, when she was the one being made to wait. She could get mad like Daddy would've, but then Auntie might make the girl disappear, and then there wouldn't be any breakfast.

At last, the girl finished, turning toward the window with the words, "Hi. What can I get— Oh … my … God." Instead of being scared, like Devon expected her to, a huge smile spread over her face. "Wow! That's, like, the best costume I've ever seen. It must have taken simply forever to make. So is there a convention in town? Because I haven't heard anything about it."

"I don't know. What's a convention?"

"What's a convention? It's a place where people who cosplay go to meet other people who cosplay. I simply love cosplay and going to conventions. I'm a wood elf when I'm not sitting here serving burgers."

Although she didn't know what cosplay was any more than she knew what a convention was, Devon knew what elves were. They were beautiful and kind and they loved everything: flowers, trees, butterflies, and unicorns. It seemed strange that an elf might be sitting here serving burgers when there was all that nature out there to be loved, but then, like God, this elf probably had her own mysterious reasons. It was best not to ask. Auntie was being good, for now. If she got mad and made an elf disappear, God might get really, really mad too. Not wanting that to happen, Devon decided she had better order instead. "Can I have a breakfast burger and milkshake, please?"

"Of course you can, sweetie. And what would your friend like?"

"Oh, she's not just my friend. She's Auntie. She's my gift from God, and she doesn't want anything because God didn't give her a mouth. I don't know why. Perhaps she just lives on sunlight like plants do."

"Um … okay. This got real weird, real fast. Sweetheart, I hope you don't mind me asking but who exactly is inside that costume?"

"Auntie is. No one listened to Jesus, so God gave her to me because he still wants everyone to be good."

"Yeah. Could you just hold on a moment? I need to go check up on something."

She disappeared, rather rapidly, and Devon decided once more that she would wait patiently for the nice elf to come back. Then she began to hear noises from inside the restaurant, voices raised in what sounded like someone was having a surprise party. Seconds later, a whole load of people appeared, all of them wearing the same uniform as the elf.

They peered out at Devon and Auntie and said, "Oh my god!" and, "What the hell?" and, "No way!" and, "Jesus, what is that?"

"She's not Jesus." Devon was somewhat surprised the elf hadn't already explained that to them. "Jesus is in Heaven with God. This is Auntie. God gave her to me."

Another woman appeared, older than the rest of them, so old, in fact, that she might be someone's gramma. Grammas usually had a way of dealing with things, and so did she. "What in the hell you all standing here gawking at? Get back to work. There are customers waiting to be served."

Then she saw Devon and Auntie. Instead of being surprised, she held them firmly in a no-nonsense gaze. "Well, ain't this just great? Someone call 9-1-1. Man, if it ain't hard enough already without fools like this getting in your face."

She left, still muttering to herself as she shooed the rest of them away. Now there was no one on the other side of the window, and that wasn't good at all. Rather disappointed, especially with the elf, who had seemed so nice, Devon looked up at Auntie. "I don't think we're going to get any breakfast here. I think we ought to go."

Back out onto the street they went and on past

houses and apartment blocks. By the time they walked by a school, Devon could hear sirens. They sounded like they were coming from everywhere, and she wondered what bad person the police could all be chasing. Eventually, in the distance, on the roads to either side, she could see them too. They were all stopped, just sitting there in their vehicles with their lights flashing, which was very strange.

"Well, they aren't going to catch any bad people like that, are they, Auntie? There could be all sorts of bad things happening while they were just sitting there, but that's okay, I guess. They must know what they're doing, and at least we know it isn't us they're looking for. If it was, they would've come and taken us away already. But then why would they do that? We haven't done anything wrong. All we did was try to order some breakfast. It was the people in the restaurant who acted all weird. Perhaps they ought to take them away before they hurt somebody."

Auntie didn't respond. She might not have even noticed. Oh well. Up ahead was a college and Devon pointed Auntie toward it.

"Let's go in there. It's like a big school so maybe they have a lunchroom."

A gap in a low wall took them across tree-scattered grass into a parking lot. People there climbed out of their cars or walked toward the college buildings—

until they saw Auntie. Then everyone stopped and stared. Some even took out their phones and took photos or made videos. That was okay. They'd send those photos to all their friends, and then lots more people would know how wonderful Auntie was. Just to make sure they all knew she was nice, too, when she wasn't getting mad, Devon waved to them as well.

Auntie ignored them and followed a path from the parking lot that took them between college buildings and then through a garden. After a bridge and some more buildings, they came to a round lawn where lots more people, all of them young and carrying either backpacks or books, sat around. They must be the students, and they looked so much happier than the people in the parking lot. Instead of staring, they smiled and laughed. Some even applauded.

One of them said, "Hey, little girl. What's the promo for?"

"Must be a video game," said another. "And that's a really awesome costume. So what's the name of the game, kid? I bet it's called Killer Alien Robot or something like that, right?"

"Dude," said the first. "That is so lame. It'll be called Silver Storm, or Stealthaggedon, or how about Metamorkosis? Yeah, that's right, because they all come down to earth, and everyone thinks they're friendly. Then they secretly start replacing all the real people with themselves, and nobody even knows they're doing it until there are just a few real humans left, and then they fight back, and eventually they free all the other real humans from wherever they're being held prisoner."

"Yeah," added a third. "So how about it, little girl? Can that thing make itself look like any one of us? Because that would be really cool, right?"

"No. That's just silly. Auntie came from Heaven and we're going to help God make everyone be nice to each other, not replace them or hold them prisoner."

At least a fourth one appeared to understand. "So it's like a game where God finally gets pissed at us, right?"

Before anyone else could say anything, the sound of approaching helicopters chopped up the quietness of the morning. Devon wasn't at all surprised when she felt the coldness of Auntie's unhappiness begin to creep through her. She already knew Auntie didn't like helicopters. Nor were they the only things to appear. While the helicopters hovered over nearby buildings, figures began to creep between them. They weren't students. With their black helmets, face masks, and the big guns they all carried, they looked a lot like robots. Devon felt sure she already knew whose robots they were, but she decided to make certain, just in case.

"Are they Nazis?"

"Damn straight," said the second student, before shouting up at the helicopters, "Hey, you fascist pigs! Why don't you go find someone else to oppress, huh?"

"Yeah," added the first. "Goddamn pigs always turning up to spoil the fun."

The helicopters weren't listening, and neither were the Nazi robots. Instead of going away and finding someone else to oppress, or at the very least not spoiling everyone's fun, a big, booming voice sounded across the entire college. "Please clear the area. You are in imminent danger. Please leave the area immediately."

Some did as they were told, but many of the rest stood gawking as if that big, booming voice was God himself. It might be, except that Auntie didn't appear to think so, and nor did many of the students standing closest to Devon. Beating the air with clenched fists, they began to chant, "Ho, ho. Hey, hey. No Nazi USA!"

Auntie was defiant too, or maybe she just didn't like someone else pretending to be God. She knew him, after all, and probably Jesus too, so nobody could really complain if she decided to get mad about it, and she did. With Devon not even trying to stop her, she froze into a deep chill and launched a green fireball at each of the helicopters. One after another the helicopters exploded, showering the Nazi robots beneath with flaming wreckage. At the sight of that, many more students left, this time running, with an awful lot of them screaming too. Those closest to Devon remained, their mouths hanging open in awe.

"No shit, dude! How in the hell did you do that?"

"Wow. I've never seen CGI close up before. That was, like, awesome."

For Devon, it was all rather ordinary. "Oh, that's just Auntie. She doesn't like Nazis either."

The robots began to disappear as well, slowly creeping back behind the buildings—a bit like crabs scuttling away in a rock pool—and Devon began to feel warm again. Auntie was happy, and so were all the students who remained. They cheered and clapped and shouted at the sky where the helicopters had been. Devon smiled at that because the world had just become a little bit nicer, and that was good.

CHAPTER
FOUR

As the cheering began to die down, one of the students asked a very good question. "So whadda we do now? I mean, we can hardly just go to class, can we?"

This was why students had to be smart, so they could ask questions like that. Of course, Devon had thought about it herself earlier, but she still didn't have an answer. Auntie had carried her thus far simply by putting one foot in front of the other, but that wasn't exactly going to make the whole world a nicer place. No. She needed somewhere to go, something to do that would make everyone sit up straight and listen. Fortunately, some of the other students did have some answers.

"We should march on city hall, right? Make Tacoma a safe space for everyone."

"Better still, let's march on the detention center and free all the undocumented. They probably got them all locked up in cages and stuff, y'know, like a concentration camp or something."

"We can do both. City hall's on the way to the detention center."

"And then we should march on Washington and take down that fascist president."

"Hell yeah! Let's take the entire country. No borders, green energy, a basic income for everyone. Let's show them all what would really make America great again."

As interesting as all that was, it was also rather confusing. Devon sort of knew what green energy was because her teachers constantly talked about it, and how horrible that fascist president was. As for the rest, well, she just had to ask. "What are the ... undocu ...?"

"The undocumented? They're people who want to come here for a better life but the racists and the Nazis won't let them in."

"That's right. They take children away from their parents and lock them up in cages."

"Well, that's not very nice. I wouldn't like that at all. Everyone should be nice to each other, kids most of all. I think we should go there and free them."

Everyone cheered. Devon was pleased because

that must mean she had made the right choice. Also, she had a whole lot of new friends, thirty or so of the students who hadn't run away. That was good because, as wonderful as Auntie might be, it was nice to have other people to talk to, people she could take care of. They would be her flock, and she would look after them, just as Jesus had tried to do. The difference would be that Auntie was there to scare the Nazis away. They were bullies, and grown-ups were wrong about bullies. Sometimes, when they'd gotten over their hurt feelings, they did come back, and then they were even nastier.

Back through the garden they went and into the parking lot, a great big carnival of happiness filling the air with chants like, "This is what democracy looks like," and, "We're all human beings," and, "No hate. No fear. Immigrants are welcome here."

The parking lot where all those people had watched Devon and Auntie was empty. The street beyond was empty too, at least to begin with. It was not hard to see why. Police vehicles lurked in the distance at every intersection. They must be directing traffic because that's what the police did when there was a carnival. It was strange that no one came out to watch, because people usually liked carnivals. They probably just didn't know. It had all happened rather suddenly, after all.

For an hour or more they walked, between houses and apartment blocks, under a bridge, and then by a school and stores. Devon kept looking for other people. She saw quite a few, but most of them stayed inside, peering out through windows or peeking from behind doors. It was almost as if they were afraid of something, which was silly. Everyone was happy and having fun. All that was missing were some flags to wave and a marching band. Others were bolder, coming out to join in with the chanting and clapping. By the time they reached the center of town, Devon's flock had grown to maybe fifty people.

Ahead of them was city hall. It looked like a big, gray castle, complete with battlements on top of its second story and a great, high tower rising above them. Devon wouldn't have been the least bit surprised if a princess waited inside to be rescued. She was probably being held prisoner by an evil witch—the exact same evil witch the unicorn killers had talked about. If so, the witch's evil guards were probably peering out through all those blank windows at the happy army that had come to demand they free the princess. Bad people didn't like happiness. It scared them so much they had to smash and destroy it, like bullies stomping on someone's school project. Devon hoped they were scared now, too scared to even whisper about how scared they were in case the evil witch heard them. If they got scared enough, they might even run away, just like the Nazi robots had done.

Well, it was a nice idea, but sadly, it wasn't to be. The doors of the castle stayed firmly shut. No matter how hard Devon's happy army hammered on them, kicked them, threw trash cans at them, and screamed to be let in, the guards wouldn't open them. They must be even more scared of the witch than Devon had thought.

Others tried to find another way in through the parking entrance. They were certain there must be one, a secret door the guards had forgotten about. If there was, they couldn't find it. The castle stood, closed and silent, and all the happy army could do was stand in the street and chant, "This is what democracy looks like."

That was sad because Devon really wanted to rescue the princess. She could probably hear them all chanting, which made it even sadder. There must be something they could do, and then it occurred to her. "What about Auntie? I'm sure she could make a way in for us."

A small number of students had stayed close-by. One of them now shook his head. "Nah. No point. They must've told everyone to leave before we got here. Let's go on to the detention center. They can't hide all those people from us."

Oh well. Rescuing lots of kids in cages was probably better than rescuing a princess, anyway, especially if she turned out to be one of those spoilt ones who always had to have everything their own way.

"Okay then. Let's do that."

On the far side of the river beyond city hall were warehouses and parking lots. It all looked rather ordinary to Devon, not at all like the kind of place there would be anyone to rescue. Eventually, they came to a long, straight road, lined on one side with trees. A long, low building sat beyond them, and most of her followers charged into its parking lot as if someone had just told them there was a whole load of chocolate bunnies hidden there. By the time she and Auntie reached the lot, they'd forced their way in. Devon didn't join them. She didn't need to. She could hear what was going on inside: the angry voices, the sounds of things being overturned and smashed.

Eventually, everything began to calm down. People sulked as they wandered out because the center was empty. All that anger and breaking things had been for nothing. There was no point in throwing a temper tantrum if no one was there to be made to feel guilty like her parents would've. Even so, Devon understood how they felt. Rescuing people was really disappointing when every time they tried there was no one there to be rescued.

"Where are they all? Did someone tell them to leave too?"

Three of her closest followers were still with her, and one of them was just as disappointed as she was.

"Must've. They guessed we were coming, so they got everyone out. So what do we do now? It's for sure we can't go round every detention center in the country, not if they're going to make everyone disappear before we even get there."

The other two were a lot more certain of themselves.

"Of course not, dude. We go to Washington. We won't need to go round every detention center in the country if we make the president release them all. For that, we need some transport: a couple of buses maybe, and a truck or something for … her."

"Like over there? There are buses and trucks parked up in that lot. Why don't we just take them?"

On hearing all of that, the disappointed one began to fill with doubt.

"Take them? But that's theft, isn't it?"

"No. That's liberation."

"You got that right, dude. Property is theft. We're just taking back what was stolen from us in the first place. Besides, what are you gonna do? Walk on over there and say pretty please? Like that's gonna work."

Devon was doubtful too, because this was

difficult. Taking things that didn't belong to you was wrong. Her parents had told her that often enough. If she understood what the others were saying, what her parents had never told her was that all the stuff they had might've been taken from other people. Her parents might've been the very people who stopped other people from having what they wanted. Then it got worse. That horrible birthday present she hadn't wanted might've been taken from someone who did want it. Auntie making them disappear might not have been such a mistake after all. God knew everything, so he must've known how her parents were lying to her.

Oh well. At least now she could start putting things right if that was what liberation meant. "Only bad people steal. Let's take them, then."

"Hell yeah! Come on, guys. Let's get everyone together and hit the road."

Calling the rest of Devon's flock together proved not to be so easy, though. Some of them weren't at all keen about going to Washington, or anywhere else, for that matter.

"I can't just take off like that. I got classes. If my grades don't improve, I might have to go work for my dad."

"No, dude, you gotta think big. Storm Washington and your teachers will give you straight A's. We might even end up running the country. What's your dad gonna say then?"

"Dunno. 'Run the country? Son, you can't even tidy your room.' Probably."

As the doubtful one squirmed, Devon tried to be helpful. "Don't you want to make all the Nazis feel sorry?" But that just made him look even more uncomfortable. "Oh well. It's okay. You don't have to come if you don't want to."

The doubtful one turned and trudged away, looking an awful lot like a scolded puppy. Devon felt sorry for him. Nice people shouldn't be made to feel ashamed, not until they started doing bad things, anyway. But then, letting Nazis get away with being bad was bad too, which was exactly what the doubtful one was doing. Quite a few others were doing it too, as they also walked away. That was sad, but it was their choice so Devon turned her back on them. She had other followers, ones who really wanted to change the world.

One of them urged the rest on. "Come on, guys. Let's go liberate some transport."

With a little over thirty left, Devon's flock crossed the road. A small warehouse and a cabin sat in the lot on the other side along with a few buses and a couple of trucks. While some tried to break into the cabin in search of keys, the rest, including Devon, turned at the sound of something roaring toward them. Devon half expected to see some terrible monster the Nazis had sent to come get her, but it was just two throaty-engined trucks. Approaching fast, they tore into the lot and slid to a halt. A dozen people jumped out of them, all dressed in black: jackets, jeans, t-shirts, and even bandannas hiding their faces. They were like a flock too, but not of cuddly white sheep. They were black sheep, or maybe even wolves, what with the way they looked at everyone else.

"Hey, Tyler." The leading one held out a hand as he approached. "I got your message, man. Thanks for thinking of us."

The follower who had called this 'liberation' greeted him.

"No sweat, dude. Couldn't start the revolution without you, could we? Hey, I want you to meet someone. This is Devon. Devon, this is Brandon. He knows all sorts of cool stuff."

Brandon was older than Tyler, taller and leaner too. They both had dark hair and brown eyes, but where Tyler's eyes were welcoming, Brandon's had a coldness to them, as if he was always just a moment away from doing something bad. Devon wasn't sure she liked him any more than she liked the wolves he'd brought with him. He smiled nicely enough, though. Okay then. If Tyler liked him, she would too, for now at least.

"Hello. This is Auntie, and we're going to make the world a nicer place so that everyone can have what they want."

"Great. That's exactly what we want too. So tell me, Devon. Where are your parents?"

"Oh, they're with God. Auntie made them disappear. She does that with people she doesn't like, unless I stop her."

"Really?" Brandon's smile faded a little as he slowly took in all of Auntie's gleaming hugeness. "I'll have to remember that." Then he quickly brightened again. "So what are you guys up to? What's the big plan?"

"Liberating some transport." Tyler glanced toward the students milling about in front of the cabin. "Yeah, we're gonna need those buses to start out for Washington, but I don't think we've found any keys yet."

"Well, don't sweat it. My guys will have them up and running soon enough. Gotta say, I haven't been on the road for quite some time. I'm looking forward to it."

Half an hour later, and just about mid-morning, their little convoy set out. The students rode in a bus with some of Brandon's people. Auntie sat next to the cab in the back of his truck, with Devon beside her on one of the two narrow benches that lined it. One of his guys sat opposite, but he didn't look very pleased about it. In fact, none of Brandon's guys looked like they were very happy about anything. They all stared, cold and sulky, like the weird kids no one wanted to play with. Devon wasn't sure what she thought of them. They might be nice and just a little bit weird, or they might be nasty. She would wait and see. If they were nice but weird, well, she wouldn't hold that against them. If they turned out to be nasty, though, she could always tell Auntie to make them disappear—if she had to.

Brandon and Tyler rode up front, with one of them driving the truck. First, they went south, and then east, passing through small towns and hamlets as the road snaked along beside a river. Whatever the Nazis were doing, Devon saw none of them, nor any police or anyone else like that. Auntie must have scared them off for good.

By midday, they reached Greenwater, a sparse community spread out along the highway with lots of trees in between its buildings. Someone decided they should stop for lunch. That was probably Brandon since he seemed to do all the deciding. He was a bossy one, for sure, but that was all right, for now.

Not having had any breakfast, Devon was more interested in how much her tummy was rumbling.

While some went to the café and others to the tavern across the way, she stayed in the back of the truck with Auntie and waited for Brandon to bring her something to eat and drink. His guy, as gloomy as a knight without a princess to rescue, went too. She was quite pleased about that.

Hardly anyone was about. The few people she did see all looked curiously at Auntie, but none of them approached. Some even shook their heads, commenting very loudly, "Damn students. Don't they have anything better to do, like going to classes?" and, "What is that thing in the back of that truck, a mascot or something?"

Devon ignored them, quietly waiting for Brandon. He returned with his hands filled with sodas and sandwiches, one of them peanut butter and jelly. While they sat opposite each other with nothing to say, Devon slowly chewed on its sticky fruitiness, happy enough to simply look at the trees lining the road and wonder what things might be hiding within them.

Brandon's gaze almost never left Auntie's unmoving hugeness, until at last he put his thoughts into words. "She is wonderful, isn't she? So where did you find her, if you don't mind me asking?"

"I don't mind. She sort of fell out of the sky. I asked God if he wanted me to make the world a nicer place, since no one had listened to Jesus and suddenly, there she was."

With a slow nod, Brandon thought some more. "And how do you talk to her? How do you tell her what to do and when to make people disappear?"

"We don't talk, not with words, anyway, but I always know when she's happy because she makes me feel all warm inside, and I know when she isn't because she makes me feel all cold inside."

"Warm and cold, huh?" Brandon paused again. He was thinking an awful lot right now. "So I guess it must be really nice when she makes you feel all warm inside. Could she make me feel all warm inside too?"

Devon shrugged. "I don't know. I think maybe she decides that. I think it probably depends on whether she likes you or not."

"Well, I guess I'd better be nice to her then, hadn't I, or she might make me disappear."

"She might have at first, but now she only makes people disappear when I tell her to, mostly."

Brandon fell into thoughtfulness again, his gaze returning to Auntie like she was a toy he really wanted. If that was what he was thinking, he was going to be disappointed. It might not be, of course, but then Devon already knew not to ask because grown-ups never owned up to stuff like that, anyway. They just pretended everything was all right, like Brandon did now, breaking into a big smile as his gaze turned back to Devon. "How about some ice cream to finish off with? Would you like that?"

"Yes, please. Chocolate chip, please."

A few minutes later, as Devon ate her ice cream, the convoy set out again. The road ran on through the trees and everything was good until Devon began to feel that chill again. Something was making Auntie unhappy. Thinking it might be more helicopters, Devon followed the turn of her head as she gazed up into the sky, but all she saw were wispy clouds in a sea of blue. It could be it wasn't Auntie at all. Eating ice cream too fast sometimes made her feel really cold inside too. After a little while, she warmed up again, so it must have been her ice cream after all.

CHAPTER FIVE

For another couple of hours, they drove, with the road climbing through a switchback and then cutting into the mountainside. The sky remained a froth-filled blue, and everything was good except for Devon's glum companion: the knight without a princess to rescue. They didn't talk, but that was all right. Devon preferred to watch the trees go by and the birds that occasionally flitted overhead, wondering every once in a while just how far it was to Washington and if they would stop again before they got there.

When they did stop, a steep slope rose above the trees to their left, and a gas station and lodge sat to their right. The bus squeaked to a halt and everyone got out. They all looked concerned, as if something really bad had just happened. Curious to know what,

Devon got out too. Leading Auntie by the hand, she wound her way to the front of the crowd that had gathered ahead of the truck, and no wonder everyone was standing there gawking. Up ahead, the slope continued, coming right down to the edge of the road. On the other side, beyond some open ground, the trees closed in on it, leaving only a narrow gap for the road to run through. Right there in that gap, some very big trucks blocked the road, and a lot of men in camouflage stood in front of them. That seemed rather selfish to Devon. They should have parked in the open area like normal people would've.

Tyler wasn't happy at all. "What do we do now?"

"We use what we've got." Brandon's dry little grin made him the only one among them who appeared to be not the least bit concerned. "All we have to do is motivate it. Whatever they are, army or National Guard, they won't last ten seconds against Auntie."

"What does motivate mean? And why are all those men blocking the road?"

Brandon's grin widened. He probably thought he was being nice, but he couldn't hide the coldness in his eyes. "Because they don't like Auntie. They want to take her away."

"But why? Auntie hasn't done anything to them."

"Because they're Nazis, just like the ones this morning. You remember them, don't you?"

Tyler sounded awfully sure. Devon wasn't so much. These men didn't look at all like those black robots at the college. Tyler and Brandon might be right, of course, but then they might not, and she didn't want to get it all wrong.

"I don't know. Shouldn't we ask them whether they're Nazis or not?"

Brandon crouched in front of her, looking all serious like grown-ups did when something was really, really important. "Listen, Devon. They're bad people. They want to take Auntie away, but you can stop them. All you have to do is tell Auntie to scare them away like she did in Tacoma."

"But they can't. God gave Auntie to me, not them."

"Well, exactly, but that doesn't mean they aren't going to try. Just tell Auntie to scare them away, and everything will be all right again."

Determinedly, Devon shook her head. "No! I'm not going to tell Auntie to scare anyone unless I'm sure they're a Nazi. And look, one of them is coming over to talk to us. I think we ought to listen, don't you? After all, they might just want to be friends, like you did."

Brandon had no answer to that. All he could do was stand and watch as a woman wearing a black pantsuit and white blouse walked toward them.

As she came closer, Devon saw she was wearing a badge. That meant she must be some kind of police or something. Brandon was even less happy about that. Auntie wasn't happy either. Devon could feel her chilling, but it wasn't this woman that Auntie was looking at. Once again, she was watching the sky, and, once again, Devon couldn't understand why. There was nothing there that she could see.

The woman arrived, and Brandon took a step forward because he thought he was in charge. "Well, look at this, guys. The fascist state has turned up to oppress us. So which part of it do you work for, lady?"

Ignoring him, and all the rest of them, she crouched in front of the person she thought was in charge. "Hi, sweetie. My name's Melissa. You must be Devon."

Devon nodded in reply. She seemed like a nice lady—not the least bit Nazi-like at all. She had shoulder-length blond hair hitched back behind her ears, so it wouldn't fall in front of her round face and hide her sparkling brown eyes and sweet smile. Devon liked her a lot more than she liked Brandon.

Melissa glanced up at the great gleaming figure towering over them all. "And who's this?"

"That's Auntie. God gave her to me."

"Really? And why did God give her to you, sweetie?"

"Because he wants me to help make the world

a nicer place."

"And did God tell you that?"

"No. But I wished for it, and then Auntie came along so it must be true."

"Devon." Brandon was all serious again. "Don't listen to her. She wants to take Auntie away from you."

Melissa glanced up at him, looking an awful lot like she didn't really like him either. "Well, sweetie, there are lots of different gods, you know, and not all of them want to make the world a nicer place."

That was a very confusing thing to say.

"But how can that be? God made everything, and he loves everyone, doesn't he?"

Brandon crouched again, his gaze as earnest as Melissa's, so that it seemed to Devon like they were somehow fighting each other for something. "That's right, Devon. God wants to make the world a nicer place. All the other gods are false, or not really gods at all, like the president. They just want to hurt people and steal everything from them. She wants to take Auntie away from you because she works for the president."

Devon said nothing. This was becoming really confusing now. No one had ever told her before that the president might be a false god. She had always been told that the president was chosen by the people to serve the people. It didn't seem right that the people would choose a false god who wanted to hurt them and steal from them. She looked up at Auntie, but that was no help at all. Now very cold indeed, Auntie was still looking at the sky, which was even more confusing.

"Devon. What happened to your parents? Did Auntie do something to them?"

"Yes." Devon looked down at her feet. Melissa was making her feel very small and guilty, which was silly because she hadn't done anything wrong. "But that was an accident, or at least I think it was. God might have told Auntie to do it, I suppose, but it's all right because now they're with him, and they're happy."

"Of course," said Brandon. "God probably told Auntie to send them to him so you wouldn't have to worry about them."

"Really!" Melissa glared at him. "You're gonna tell this kid God killed her parents because they were an inconvenience?"

"And what are you going to tell her, huh? That she pretty much killed them herself?"

Melissa pointed at Auntie. "No. That thing killed them. It's a danger to everyone on this planet, including her. Look at her. She's a child. She believes what she's told to believe. Priest or educator; it doesn't matter. She believes God gave her that thing and that every person it kills ends up in some happy place. Doesn't that disturb you at all? Doesn't that just scare the hell out of you?"

Now Brandon was glaring too. "What scares the hell out me is what you're going to tell her to believe. Yeah, she's a child, but so what? Sometimes it takes that kind of innocence to make us see the truth. If she can make the world a nicer place where people like you have all failed, if you ever even really tried, I'm up for it, and if sacrifices have to be made along the way, so what? When have you and the people you work for ever shied away from sacrificing others to get what you want?"

They were starting to shout at each other. Devon didn't like it when people shouted at each other, especially when she didn't understand what they were shouting about. She didn't know how to stop them either, so all she could do was stand and watch.

Melissa let slip a bitter laugh.

"Oh please! Don't try to dress yourself up as some kind of woke saint. She thinks that thing's a gift from God because she doesn't know any better. You think that thing's a gift from God—if you even believe in God—because you think that thing is your ticket to power, and that's all you're really interested in. You don't want to create a nicer world. You just want to control it, and you think you'll get there by controlling her."

"And you don't? Just think, there's a whole world out there you could remake in your own image because that's what everyone wants, right, to be just like us? All you gotta do is make her believe it's what God wants too. Hell, you could probably take over the entire planet in a week."

They stood and glared at each other even more coldly than Auntie. Devon wished she would stop looking at the empty sky. She wanted these people to stop fighting, but not only had Auntie not even noticed, she also wasn't listening to Devon's wishing.

"And that makes us different how? At least we believe in freedom. What do you believe in? A society in which everyone is equal: equally dependent, equally mind-controlled, and equally demonized if they don't comply. Everyone except for those at the top, of course. Everyone except for you!"

"Stop it! Stop it!" Devon had listened enough. She still didn't understand what they were arguing about. It all just sounded silly to her. There was one thing she did understand, though, and she was going to make them understand it too. "Auntie is mine! God gave her to me! Neither of you can have her!"

Both of them looked down at her. Melissa began to say, "Devon—"

"No!" Devon had made her mind up, and she'd decided she didn't like Melissa so much anymore. "You better go now. Auntie is very unhappy. She might do something you won't like at all."

She might if she would only stop watching the sky. The threat was enough to have Melissa looking all hurt, though. "Well, I'm sorry to hear that, Devon, but I'm afraid it doesn't make any difference. This little road trip of yours is over. You will all surrender yourselves, and that, to us, now!"

Brandon wore a wicked grin. "Or what? You're gonna shoot us all?"

"Maybe. After all, who's gonna know any different? There's no one here but us, and the media will say what we tell them to say. So maybe there was a terrible accident on a high mountain road. A bus and a truck collided, and everyone died before help could arrive."

"Right. So it's Operation Mockingbird, and you work for the company. You see, Devon? She works for a bad god. It's called the CIA, and they just want Auntie for themselves."

Devon tugged urgently on Auntie's huge silver fist. Melissa was about to do something, and Devon was afraid Brandon might be right. Melissa was going to try to take Auntie away. Even now, she was retreating a few steps so she could talk to everyone else.

"You all heard your glorious leader. So who wants to sacrifice themselves for him? Anyone? Who wants to die so he can make himself Chairman of the People's Republic of Brandon? How about you girls? You wanna be at his beck and call for whatever he chooses to demand of you? Some equality that'll be, right? Or you can listen to me because I'm on your side. Give it up now and you'll be back in Tacoma in time for supper. No record will be made of this. Your parents will never know, and that will be the end of it. All you have to do is walk away now."

An awful lot of glances were exchanged, mostly among the students. While Brandon's guys looked to him and stood firm, one by one the students began to walk. Tyler tried to stop them, but Melissa's words were working. Devon's little flock was whittled away until there was little more than a dozen left.

Again, she tugged on Auntie's fist, willing her to stop daydreaming, and then suddenly she did. Raising her other hand, she shot a green bolt into the sky. Devon gasped as she watched it streak silently heavenward. At first, it flew straight as an arrow. Then it veered and weaved as if it was chasing something. Finally, it exploded into a great black and white shower as though some huge firework had just gone off.

"Everybody get down! Now!"

Devon spun round. Melissa stood with her legs apart, the gun in her hand pointed squarely at Auntie. Behind her, the men in camouflage all rushed forward, their guns raised and ready to fire. Just about everyone else lay flat on the road. Only Brandon wasn't. Hunkered down with the spread fingertips of one hand touching the pavement, he watched with a huge grin on his face, a grin that turned to open laughter as Auntie turned too. No longer interested in the sky, she raised both her hands. Before she could do anything more, Melissa fired off several rounds. Devon saw them pancaked into little depressions in Auntie's chest. Fascinated, she watched as they were slowly pushed out to fall to the pavement, leaving behind not even the slightest mark on Auntie's silvered skin. At the same time, red balls flew from the blunt end of one finger on each hand. Melissa and all the men in camouflage glowed and hissed and disappeared. From another finger, blue balls followed, and the vehicles blocking the road up ahead crunched and squealed and disappeared too.

Silence followed, a dead hush as if the entire world was holding its breath. It was broken by an excited Brandon pumping his fist in the air and shouting some very bad words. Everyone else crawled to their feet, looking shaken, scared, even. Of course, the students had seen Auntie destroy the helicopters over the college, but Brandon's guys hadn't. This was also the first time any of them had seen Auntie make people disappear, and now Brandon's guys looked like they were the most scared of all.

Auntie was warming rapidly. Whatever the firework had been, she was happy again now it was gone, and so was Devon. Everything was good again, apart from Melissa. She hadn't really been a bad person. She had just been serving a bad god, and Devon did feel a little sorry for her.

As for everyone else, Brandon and Tyler moved among them, calming them down and trying to cheer them up. No one seemed very happy; the ones who had started to walk away least of all. Now that all the excitement was over, though, she was more interested in the lodge. She'd had some ice cream not so very long ago. Having some more too soon wasn't good, or so her parents always said, but she surely deserved some kind of reward. She had done what they wanted, after all. Well, Auntie had done what they wanted, so it was only fair. Maybe she would say so when Brandon and Tyler had finished talking to each other. But when Tyler came over to talk to her, he looked terribly serious and she forgot about it.

"Devon. Do you know what a drone is?"

She shook her head.

"Okay. Well, a drone is like a plane, only it doesn't have a pilot. It can do everything a plane can do, though, like blowing things up. We think that thing Auntie shot at in the sky was a drone. We think Melissa, or the bad god CIA, had been using it to follow us all the way from Tacoma. We think Melissa was trying to draw us away from Auntie so that the drone could kill her."

"Kill her? But I thought the bad god CIA wanted her for itself. Isn't that what Brandon said?"

"Well, yes. Brandon did say that, but then Brandon isn't always right. Sometimes he gets it completely wrong and, the truth is, we don't really know what they meant to do. Maybe they were going to take her away. Maybe they were going to kill her."

"So why didn't the bad god CIA just kill Auntie before she killed its drone?"

"We don't know. We think maybe it was because Melissa didn't want to hurt you. Bad gods can make people do bad things, but only for so long as those people are willing to do them. We think Melissa didn't want to. So we want you to make us a promise. You'll never leave Auntie's side, not for a moment, and we will never leave yours. That way, if the bad god CIA sends someone else, maybe they won't want to hurt you either. Can you do that for us, Devon? Can you help keep Auntie safe?"

Well, that was an easy promise to make since Auntie would do whatever Devon told her to do, mostly. So of course she would never leave Auntie's side, and Auntie would never leave hers. "Okay. Pinkie swear?"

"Pinkie swear."

Tyler curled his little finger around hers, and then he was gone, returning to where Brandon was calling everyone together. Many of them were still unhappy, with little glances and murmurs being passed between them that said how much they wanted to go home.

Brandon knew it as well as Devon did, but he wasn't going to give up on them just like that. "Okay, guys, this is it. I know a lot of you weren't expecting this, but here it is anyway. This is the new revolution and, like the old revolution, we either win together or we hang together. So let's stick together and win it, yeah? Let's get on over there to Washington and take down all the corrupt politicians, the casino bankers, and all of the other white oppressors. Let's show everyone what will really make this country great again. We have nothing to lose but our chains, comrades, so are you with me?"

There was a rather halfhearted chorus of approval, but that only made Brandon even more determined. "Oh come on, you can do better than that. You're the new founding ... um ..."

"Gender nonspecific persons," suggested someone.

"Guardians," suggested another. "Or how about heroes of the revolution."

"That's right. You're the new founding heroes of the revolution. You'll have statues raised and high schools named after you. Professors will write books about you. Hell, they'll probably even make a miniseries. Forget George Washington and Benjamin Franklin and all those other old white males. It'll be your faces everyone sees when they pay for something. So come on, comrades. Gimme a hell yeah, and let's get this show on the road."

That brought a better response, enough at least to get everyone back on the bus. Brandon stood and watched, satisfied enough to be wearing that grin of his again. Devon still thought she didn't like him very much, but he seemed to know what they should be doing. She would just have to watch out for when she thought he was doing it wrong. God wouldn't have sent him to her unless he wanted him to be there, but that didn't mean she was going to let him do whatever he wanted.

CHAPTER SIX

The road continued alongside the river, with bare hillsides and stands of trees giving way to fields and the small town of Naches. The next large town they came to was Yakima. They came in off the first exit, crossed over a wide junction, and pulled off the highway in front of a restaurant. Devon was pleased. It was almost an hour since the lodge and three hours since they'd left Greenwater. That was a very long time to be sitting in the back of a truck with no one but Auntie and the glum knight to talk to. Also, since she'd done what Brandon wanted her to do, he still owed her a reward.

Well, maybe later.

Brandon leaped out of the truck, only interested in the van parked in the restaurant lot. A man and a woman stood before its open door. The man was young, not much older than Tyler, and casually, almost carelessly dressed. Straggling hair poked out from under a woolen hat pulled down almost to his eyebrows, and he was also holding a very big camera. The woman, somewhat older, with short, black hair, was smartly dressed in a dark blue jacket and skirt, and she looked very, very stern.

In her right hand she held a microphone. Large letters ending in TV were written on the side of the van.

After reading them, the glum knight became even glummer. "Local TV? What the hell is local TV doing here?"

Tyler overheard as he followed Brandon out of the truck. "Chill, dude. Brandon called them. You can't have a revolution without going public, and the state controls national TV. What better way to reach the people than going local? Once we're out there, maybe the state'll think twice about coming after us again."

The glum knight snorted, and Devon wondered if there was anything that might cheer him up.

Meanwhile, the rest of Devon's flock poured off the bus as well, and Devon watched as Brandon approached the woman with an outstretched hand. "Hey, thanks for coming. I thought you might be interested."

"Yeah well, we weren't going to. My boss thought you were just another crank call until we started getting a whole lot of others asking if we knew what this weird little convoy heading in our direction was all about. My name's Ali, by the way, and this is my cameraman, Ross. So, Brandon, before we start shooting, perhaps you'd give us the lowdown on exactly what this is all about?"

"Sure. So we think this country is headed in entirely the wrong direction. Like, whatever happened to the city on the hill? It got hijacked is what, by greed and corruption and exploitation and those that could grab everything for themselves. So we're going to Washington, and we're going to make this country what it was meant to be: a place where everybody gets an equal share, and nobody gets to play god with other people's lives."

Ali nodded, slow and thoughtful. "Right. So you're just gonna head on over to DC and change the world, huh? Well, that's pretty ambitious, I'll grant you that. It's a long way from here to there, though, and, somehow, I don't think a whole lotta people over there are gonna see it that way. Does that not bother you at all?"

"Nah. We got a secret weapon. C'mon, I want you to meet someone." Too full of himself to notice Ali's doubt, Brandon led her and Ross over to the back of the truck. "This is Devon. She's sort of our inspiration. Out of the mouths of babes and sucklings, right? We should listen to kids like her because her generation will have to live with what we leave behind. And this is Auntie. She's, like, Devon's guardian, I suppose."

"You suppose?" Ali looked at Devon. Then she looked at Auntie. What she thought of her, Devon couldn't tell, but she wouldn't have been in the least surprised if someone was about to get a scolding. It would be rather unfair if it was Auntie because she was just sitting there, on the warm side of neutral and not in the least bit interested in any of them.

Fortunately, Ali must have thought better of it. Instead of scolding anyone, Auntie in particular, she burst into a quick, bright smile. "Hey. So you're Devon, are you? Well, it's really great to meet you. So what's a pretty little girl like you doing out here with all these grown-up boys?"

"Oh, nothing right now. But later, we're going to see the president, and we're going to tell him to stop being nasty to people."

"Really? And this is Auntie, is it? Wow, that's a really super costume she's wearing. Do you think she might take that helmet off so I could ask her some questions?"

Devon shook her head. "No."

"No! Why? Doesn't she want to talk to me?"

"Auntie only talks to me and, right now, I don't think she's very interested in you."

"Okay. Well, does Auntie have a name, at least?"

"No. She's just Auntie. She looks after me now that my parents are with God."

"Your parents are with God!" Ali's smile collapsed as if she'd just bitten into an apple and found a worm. Well, that was horrible for sure, but it had nothing to do with Devon's parents being with God. Being with God was a good thing, but now Ali was looking at Brandon and Tyler as if it wasn't and they were responsible for it. They weren't, and neither was Auntie so long as her mistake hadn't really been a mistake. Still, as she returned to Devon, Ali wasn't happy at all. "So, sweetie, who's responsible for you? Is there someone I can call who knows you're here? At the very least, shouldn't you be in school?"

"No."

"No! All I'm getting here is no. At least tell me the rest of your name, unless they've told you not—"

"Her name is Devon. I already told you that. And, believe me, no one's going to harm her while Auntie's around. Now, come on. There are a lot more of us on the bus and, despite what you're thinking, they're not all guys."

As Brandon walked away, Ali muttered, "Yeah, right. Because no woman has ever been convicted of abusing a child, have they?"

Ross replaced her, his big camera pointed at Devon and Auntie. He must've quietly recorded them the whole time. That was a bit sneaky of him, but Devon was far more interested in something else. "Are we going to be on TV?"

"Probably. Why don't you give me a big smile and a wave just so everyone can see how happy you are?" Once she'd done that, Ross turned the camera onto Auntie. "And how about Auntie? Can she give me a wave too?"

Devon shook her head. For all she knew, Auntie waving might lead to Auntie making people disappear. Auntie was quite happy sitting there minding her own business, and Devon was quite happy to leave her be.

Hardly noticing the refusal, Ross panned the camera across to the glum knight. Devon still didn't know his name. She didn't really feel like finding out either, and nor did Ross. Having recorded as much glumness as anyone could possibly want, he quickly followed Ali to where Brandon was introducing everyone off the bus, leaving only Tyler standing beside the truck.

As he watched Ross go, the glum knight said, "Great! Genius! I swear, sometimes Brandon is too clever for his own good."

"Meaning?"

"Meaning transporting a minor across state lines is a federal offense. He has to go and invite a reporter here, a female one at that, and now she thinks we're child trafficking or something. Way to go, Brandon."

Tyler chuckled. "Lighten up, dude. You heard what he said. So long as Auntie's here, no one's going to lay a finger on her, or us for that matter, and that includes the federal authorities. That reporter can think what she likes. Brandon will win her over. He's good at that sort of thing. You'll see."

"What's child trafficking?" asked Devon.

Tyler and the glum knight looked at each other, like neither of them quite knew what to say, until Tyler replied, "It's um … it's when people take kids to places they don't want to go."

"Oh. So it's a bit like making kids go to school, then."

Tyler grinned and walked away. "You can answer that one."

The glum knight snorted. He snorted at everything, but that was okay. Devon didn't really expect him to answer. What he needed was a princess to rescue. Then he might fall in love and stop being so glum. That wasn't going to happen, though, not if the Nazis kept making all the princesses disappear like they had in Tacoma. Oh well. Devon looked over to the bus instead. All her flock stood there behind Brandon, and Ali stood in front of him, the two of them talking to each other in turns, while Ross stood back a little, recording it all.

Beyond, little huddles of onlookers began to gather, curious as to what was going on. Mostly, they were curious about Auntie. Lots of phones came out, so they could shoot their own videos of her. Devon was pleased they were all so interested. The more people saw Auntie, the more they might like her. The more they liked her, the more they might listen, and then the more they might start being nice to each other.

At last, the interview ended, which was good. Devon was becoming bored. While the rest of her flock got back on the bus, Brandon went to talk to some of the onlookers. Ross followed, still recording everything, and Ali returned to the back of the truck. Though unhappy before, now she wore an easy smile, as if Brandon had explained to her how there really was nothing to be worried about.

"Well, it looks as though we're coming with you, sweetie, at least for a little while. What do you think of that?"

"I think it's good. Then you can show everyone how we just want to make the world a nicer place."

"Absolutely, because who wouldn't want that, right?"

"Nazis. And bad gods."

"Sweetheart, do you even know who the Nazis were?"

Devon nodded. "They're people who don't want other people to be happy or have what they want."

Ali fell silent, casting a glance toward the glum knight. She must be expecting him to say something. He didn't, which Devon, at least, was pleased about. If he'd said something, it would probably have been something gloomy, and no one wanted to be friends with the sulky kids.

Ali must have felt that way too because she abruptly turned and walked away. Halfway toward her van, she stopped and took out her phone. She spoke to someone, and the conversation grew increasingly heated, her free hand waving about ever more excitedly. Whoever it was mustn't have liked what she said or wouldn't give her what she wanted. Melissa had worked for a bad god. It could be that Ali worked for a bad god too or maybe even a Nazi. If she did, Devon wouldn't tell Auntie. Ali seemed like she was nice, like Melissa had, at the start, anyway, and Devon didn't want Auntie to make her disappear, not until she'd decided either way.

Meanwhile, Brandon had persuaded a handful of the onlookers to get on the bus. The rest walked away, some shaking their heads, others openly laughing, just like the people in Greenwater had done. If they made comments as well, Devon couldn't hear them, but then she wasn't very interested. These people would probably have laughed at Jesus too and not been the least bit sorry about it when he died. Besides, Ross now ambled over to Ali. She waved at him to hurry up, but he continued to amble, which only made her wave at him all the more. When he was close enough, she thrust the phone at him, then stood with arms firmly folded while he talked to whoever she'd been speaking to. It was a short conversation, little more than a series of nods on Ross's part.

At the same time, Brandon returned to the truck, wearing another satisfied grin. "So we got us a few more followers. Now we need to move on to the next town and maybe pick up some more."

The glum knight nodded toward Ali and Ross. "And they're coming with us, are they?"

"Yeah. You got a problem with that? Hey, the more people we have, the less they can do to stop us. That's what having the media on your side can do for you. It will also make them think twice about using troops against us. What's not to like about that?"

"Oh, I don't know. How about Auntie going apeshit on the lot of them for all the world to see?"

"But that's not going to happen, is it? Because we're Auntie's friends, and Devon won't let her do that, will you?" As Devon shook her head, Brandon continued, "There you are, then. Now, come on. We need to find somewhere to spend the night—unless, of course, you're getting cold feet."

"No! I just don't want people looking at me like I'm some kind of kiddy fiddler, that's all. You do know what they do to people like that in the slammer, don't you?"

"Well, we aren't going to have to worry about that, now, are we? The real kiddy fiddlers are over there in Washington, and they're the ones going to the slammer. As for our pet reporter over there, just be nice. She's almost as important as Devon and Auntie." With a glance at Devon, Brandon added, "Perhaps you ought to go ride in the bus. You can sit at the back and feel as sorry for yourself as you want."

"Suits me."

The glum knight leaped from the back of the truck and stamped away. Brandon shook his head as he watched him go.

"Tyler can ride out here with you and Auntie from now on. I'm sure he'll be better company."

Devon nodded. She wasn't at all sorry to see the glum knight go and, just as Brandon said, Tyler was much better company. The convoy moved on, with Ali and Ross's van bringing up the rear, and he did his best to keep her entertained. He was good at that, and

Devon liked playing games with him, but sometimes even he ran out of things to say and do. Then they just watched together as they continued alongside the river, passing by more small towns and farmland.

For nearly two hours they traveled, the silences growing longer, little by little. By the time they'd passed by Richland and Kennewick, the silence had grown very long and Devon grew bored. She also felt hungry again. "I want something to eat."

"So do I." Tyler slid open the window in the back of the cab and stuck his head through. For what seemed like forever, he remained that way. When he finally returned to sit down opposite her again, all that came of it was, "Looks like we're going to have to wait a little longer."

Well, that was no good. Devon rose, determinedly lurching her way toward the front of the truck. Tyler reached out a helping hand, but she ignored it, steadying herself on Auntie's silver knees instead. Some people just had to be told, that was all. Sticking her head through the window, she told Brandon, "We're hungry. We want to stop."

Glancing at her from behind the wheel, he smiled like he always did. "When we stop for the night, okay? It'll be another hour or so. You can wait that long, can't you?"

"No! We want to stop now. You don't want to

make Auntie mad, do you?"

He glanced at her again, not smiling anymore. One of his guys sat in the cab with him, and he wasn't smiling either. He stared out the passenger side window at the passing scenery, not wanting any part in an argument. He might even be a little scared, like the girl at the fire in the forest, and all those people outside the restaurant in Belfair. Devon had almost forgotten about them. Now that she remembered, she began to see something she'd sort of only half-understood before. It was a really big something, and it was going to need some really big thinking about.

Brandon must have been thinking about it too because now he sighed. "Okay. Okay. We'll stop at the next town, all right?"

"Good. Now we can all be happy again."

Well, Devon was happy, and if she was happy, everyone else ought to be happy too. She returned to sit next to Auntie.

"So what's happening?"

Tyler's question went unanswered. The something Devon had to think about was far more important. Auntie was scary. Not everyone was scared of her straight away. They had to see her make someone disappear first. Once they did, they pretty much did anything she told them to do. That was like being a real princess, with a real kingdom and a palace and an army full of brave soldiers and lots and lots of people who would love her because she'd made them happy. Well, she didn't actually have any of that yet, but never mind. Making all of it become real must be how she was meant to make the world a nicer place. That was what she would do, then, because that was what God wanted.

CHAPTER SEVEN

After crossing the Columbia River, they drove into Umatilla and found a restaurant and truck stop. In the parking lot, everyone piled out of the bus, and then stood around as if they needed someone to tell them what to do. Devon stayed in the back of the truck with Auntie, happy enough to let Brandon continue to pretend he was in charge, even if he did sound a tiny bit mad.

"So?" he said. "I thought everyone wanted to eat. Well, there's the restaurant. What are you waiting for?"

It fell to Tyler to explain. "I think everyone's sort of wondering who's paying for it. Most of us didn't have that much on us to start with, y'know, and it's a long way to Washington. So who's paying for all of this?"

Brandon looked even madder, like he was about

to throw a tantrum. Or he simply hadn't thought of that yet, which was rather silly because even Devon knew stuff had to be paid for. Well, it did unless Auntie scared people into handing it over for free. Devon wasn't about to do that, though, not this time. No. This was for Brandon to figure out, and he better do it soon, before people started to think maybe he wasn't so smart after all. His answer to all those expectant faces was to look to Ali, but she wasn't about to bail him out either.

"No way, Che. My boss said we could come along and record the story. He didn't say we were paying for any of it."

That left Tyler to ask again. "So who's paying? People need to eat. People need somewhere to sleep. The bus and the trucks need gas. So who's paying for it all?"

"Well … why should anyone pay? All resources should be shared equally, right? So perhaps it's time the big corporations that own these places gave something back."

"Oh, right." Ali nodded, with a smile she might have stolen from Brandon. "So you just want to walk in there and take whatever you want. What about all the people who work there? Your revolution is going to be built on depriving them of their livelihood, is it?"

"No! Of course not! In the perfect society, everyone will contribute as they're able and be given according to their need. In the meantime, until we achieve perfection, sacrifices may be required."

"Great. So you're paying, then." When Ali's insistence failed to move Brandon, she added, "What? Sacrifices may be required; isn't that what you just said? Well, here's your chance to lead by example. You do have money, don't you, or at least a credit card? You want those people to work for everyone else's benefit, so how about you? You do have a job, don't you?"

"Of course I have a job. I'm an activist. My job is to campaign to make society fairer for everyone."

"Right. So basically you live in your mom's basement. She cooks all your meals and does all your laundry, and your parents pay for everything."

"No! I have a trust fund and my own apartment. No one ever changed the world by spending all their time flipping burgers or working in a call center. Hell, half the founding fathers lived on plantations worked by slaves, and it wasn't any of them who signed the declaration of independence."

By the time Brandon finished, Ali wasn't listening anymore. She was too busy laughing. "Oh yeah, I should've guessed. You're just another poor little rich kid that no one understands."

Tyler wasn't too impressed either. "You have a trust fund? When were you going to tell the rest of us?"

"Well, now, I guess. Hey, it's not my fault my parents were capitalist exploiters. I'm just trying to put things right here, y'know."

"Well isn't that great," said Tyler, with a smirk. "So you're paying, then."

"That's right! I'm paying. So come on everyone. The burgers are on me."

With that, Brandon stalked away, about as happy as the glum knight on a good day. For the next hour, Devon stayed outside in the back of the truck with Auntie. Everyone else went inside, except for Tyler, who brought something out for her. As they sat together eating, people wandered by. Some of them stopped to talk, and the conversation was almost always the same.

"Wow, neat costume. So what are you all up to? Some kind of protest or something?"

"Yeah, we're going to Washington and maybe wake some people up along the way."

"Really? Well, good luck with that. And good luck to whoever's inside that thing. It must be pretty uncomfortable having to wear that all day."

"Oh, she's fine. It's all mod cons in there, like a real NASA spacesuit. Don't tell 'em but we stole all their designs when we built it."

"Well, hey, why not? Our tax dollars paid for it, so why shouldn't we? It's sort of our property anyway, right? Okay then. We'll keep an eye out for you on the news."

Unlike Brandon, who was probably still sulking somewhere inside the restaurant, Tyler made no attempt to recruit anyone. He was quite happy just to talk to people and be nice so that when these passersby walked away, they all walked away happy. Devon liked that, and she began to like Tyler a whole lot more, more than she liked Brandon, anyway. Tyler was on the chubby side, with a puppyish enthusiasm that hardly ever flagged. If he had a tail, Devon just knew he'd constantly wag it. Brandon was completely the opposite, more like one of those angry dogs that wouldn't stop barking unless you gave them something to chew on. Yes. Out of the two of them, Tyler was definitely her favorite.

Back on the road, the early evening brought them to Baker City and a motel to the east of town in among a sprawl of businesses and warehouses. This time, Brandon didn't cause a scene. He simply paid for everything, then quietly went away to share a room with one of his guys. Devon, it was decided, would share a room with Ali. Auntie came with them, just about managing to squeeze herself through the door.

Last night, she had walked all night, carrying the

sleeping Devon in her arms. Tonight she stood in a corner, like some suit of armor in a museum. Perhaps she was tired after all that walking and had gone to sleep already. Devon couldn't tell. All she knew was that Auntie was neither happy nor mad. She was simply there, like the two beds with a nightstand between them and the dresser opposite with a TV on top.

That left only Ali to talk.

"So, sweetie. You must be a very tired little girl. Perhaps we should get you ready for bed. Do you have any PJs or something to brush your teeth with?"

Devon shook her head.

"Well now, we're going to have to do something about that, aren't we?" After a moment's thought, Ali added, "Do you have any other clothes at all?"

Again, Devon shook her head.

"You mean to tell me they've brought you all the way here from Tacoma without once even thinking of getting you a change of clothes. My god. Men! Or should I say boys? If it isn't all flashing lights and loud noises, they haven't got a clue what to do with it. And what about anyone else? Who let them drag you all the way here with nothing more than the clothes you're wearing? You said your parents were with God. So who's supposed to be looking after you?"

"Auntie. She's been looking after me ever since

she made my parents disappear."

"What?" Ali glanced toward the great silver statue that was Auntie, standing there in the corner with her head almost touching the ceiling. "Are you telling me that thing killed your parents?"

Devon shrugged. "Sort of, I guess. But she wouldn't have done it unless God wanted her to. Or maybe it was an accident. It probably was an accident because, back then, she didn't understand like she does now. I think she thought they were going to hurt me. She knows better now. She only makes people disappear when I tell her to, mostly."

Ali crouched down in front of her.

"Sweetheart. Don't you understand? That thing kills people."

"Only Nazis. And people who serve bad gods, like Melissa."

"Melissa? Who's Melissa?"

"She tried to stop us coming to meet you. She worked for the bad god CIA so Auntie made her and all the soldiers with her disappear. She also blew up a ... a drone, and some helicopters in Tacoma because they were trying to stop us coming as well."

Ali rose again, turning to stare at Auntie with a hand to her mouth. She was thinking again, and Devon waited for her to finish, kicking her feet against the bed. There was nothing else to do, what with

Auntie being asleep. Apart from occasional sounds from the rooms to either side, there was silence, and Devon thought about turning the TV on because this was boring. Maybe there'd be some cartoons or something. She liked cartoons.

Then Ali's hand dropped from her mouth. "Of course. That light aircraft that crashed earlier today. That was the drone. And then there was that incident in Tacoma that Brandon said was just a promo gone wrong. That was Auntie too, wasn't it?" She turned to face Devon, crouching before her again. "Sweetheart, where are you from?"

"California. My daddy owns his own company, or at least he did. Do I own it now?"

"Devon, what were Mommy and Daddy's names?"

"Mark and Sarah Donahoe. We were staying up by our lake when Auntie arrived."

"Yes. The news said you were all on a retreat somewhere in Asia when something happened up there. Except, of course, you weren't, so that was fake news. And then the internet went wild with claims that an alien spaceship had crashed. All totally ridiculous, of course. Nobody but wackos and nutjobs would believe … Oh my god! No way!" Ali turned sharply to look at Auntie some more. "That thing is alien?"

"No. Auntie is a gift from God so that I can help make the world a nicer place."

"No, sweetheart, that thing isn't from God. That thing is from outer space. You know, like in the TV shows."

"But they're all made up. Auntie is real. You can't just make stuff up and then it becomes real."

"Oh, believe me, you can. Grown-ups do it all the time or, at least, people who think they're grown-ups. I know. I work with them."

"Yes, grown-ups can be silly like that, like when they say boys can be girls. Everyone knows boys are far too stupid to be girls. That's why Auntie has to be a girl, because she's not stupid at all."

"Well, there is that, I suppose. But Devon, she's also dangerous. You know she makes people disappear. What if, one day, she just suddenly decides to make you disappear because, I don't know, maybe she doesn't want to be your friend anymore?"

"Don't be silly. We'll always be friends. Right from when we first met, she made me feel all warm and happy inside. Now we know how both of us are feeling all the time, which is how friends should be, isn't it?"

"All the time? Are you telling me you're somehow connected to her? Even if you left, she would still know where you are?"

Devon shrugged. "Probably. I don't know. All I know is she makes me feel happy, and we're going to be best friends forever."

Ali didn't reply. She seemed a little lost. Devon couldn't think why. She'd explained it all as best she could. Maybe Ali just couldn't think of anything to say. That must be it because then she said, "Well, we'll talk about this again tomorrow. For now, it really is time for bed. So come along, sweetheart, let's get you all tucked in."

The next morning, everyone met up next to the bus. Once again, most of them seemed to be waiting for someone else to tell them what to do. That was usually Brandon's job. Before he could say anything, though, Ali fixed him with a 'we're getting to the bottom of this right now' kind of stare, just like Mommy used to when she was about to start a fight. "How long have you known?"

Brandon clearly recognized it. Just like Daddy, he tried to play all innocent. "How long have I known what?"

Ali pointed at Auntie. "What that thing is."

"Sorry. You've lost me. What do you think that thing is?"

"Oh, come on! Are you seriously going to stand there and tell me you didn't realize almost instantly that that thing is alien?"

Brandon looked around at all the faces watching, his expression inviting them to find Ali's words ridiculous. They remained blank, for now. "Alien? Really?"

"Yeah, really. What else could it be?"

"Oh, I don't know. How about a secret weapon that maybe escaped from Area 51?"

"Area 51. You mean that place that's supposed to be full of alien technology?"

Brandon glanced at the others a second time, like a schoolyard bully trying to gee up his hangers-on. "Well, why not? I don't know about alien technology. I've never been to Area 51, but it's probably all just a lie, a cover-up to hide all those things they don't want us to know about, like weather weapons and EMP bombs. Just think about it. When has our government ever not lied to us?"

"Yeah," said one of his guys. "Like the Kennedy assassination."

"Or the moon landings," said a second.

"Or WMDs in Iraq," added a third.

Ali laughed. "Oh my god. Can you people even hear yourselves? You're using conspiracy theories to debunk a conspiracy theory."

Those few voices were enough support for Brandon, though. "Maybe. But here's the thing. Most conspiracy theories are lies. That's one of the ways they control us. Seriously. They do something dirty, like blow up the twin towers. They know they can't hide the truth forever, so they create a whole load of conspiracy theories, half of which contradict the other half. New theories come along that are even more ridiculous than the old ones and, before you know it, everybody's laughing at them, and that's when you release the truth because, by then, no one's gonna believe it anyway. It's just another conspiracy theory.

"Which is what this is. Just another conspiracy theory. Come on guys, you're not actually buying this, are you?"

"Why not?" said someone. "It's better than anything you've come up with."

"Besides which," continued Brandon, "I did say most conspiracy theories; not all. And I demonstrated how those conspiracy theories can be used to hide the truth. So what have you got? Some friendly passing aliens gave a seven-year-old kid a fully functioning robot because, y'know, that's what they do? So what's more likely, guys? That, or that our government built Auntie alongside all their stealth tanks and stealth planes and, somehow, she got out. Now they want her back, and that right there is when karma kicks in, because now we got her, and she's gonna help us overthrow them. Am I right or am I right?"

"Yeah, man," came the chorus of support. "You got it right, bro," and, "Sounds good to me."

"Oh, please. Now he's using a conspiracy theory to make everything else look like a conspiracy theory.

Can't you guys see that?"

"Of course they can, because that's what I've been saying all along. But hey, if you want to put one conspiracy up against another, I'm good with that. Let's take a vote, because this is a democracy, right? So how many—"

"Only when you think you've already won."

Dismissing Ali's comment with a smirk, Brandon continued, "So how many people think some friendly passing aliens gave Auntie to Devon as a birthday present?"

Not one single hand went up.

"And how many people think our own government built Auntie, probably to use against us?"

Every hand went up. While Brandon grinned triumphantly, Ali could only stand there and shake her head. As for Devon, she stood hand-in-hand with Auntie, silently watching it all and wondering why no one was asking her. She knew exactly where Auntie came from, and so did Auntie herself, if only she had a voice to say it with. God should have thought of that, but then he probably had his own reasons for not doing so.

CHAPTER EIGHT

"Okay, everyone." Brandon was brimming with confidence now he thought he had Ali beat. "Let's mount up and get moving. We'll find somewhere to eat along the way."

"No, we won't." Devon recognized the determined tone in Ali's voice. She wasn't beaten after all, and Brandon had better start listening, if he knew what was good for him. "We're going into town. We can eat there."

"And why would we do that?"

"Because Devon's been wearing the same clothes for god only knows how long. Days, at least, I'd guess. She needs some new ones. If you weren't so wrapped up in yourself, maybe you would have recognized that by now. There's other stuff we need as well, and not just for Devon either. There are a lot of people here with nothing but the clothes they're standing up in. A good leader would have already taken care of that."

"Oh, I'm sorry, only I've been rather busy lately."

"Yeah. So is the president, I'll bet. You wanna run the country, but you can't even look after a kid or your own followers, for that matter. So what say we ask Devon, since she's the one who's friends with Auntie? What would you like to do, Devon? Would you like to go to town? We'll get you some nice new clothes and something to eat."

"Um." Devon pretended to think hard, just like Ali did, although she already knew what she wanted to do. "I think … we'll go into town."

Ali grinned. Brandon glared. His jaw moved from side to side like he was chewing his way through a whole series of smart replies. While each one turned sour on his tongue, Tyler and Ross approached. They'd shared a room last night and now they talked together like best friends. Devon was doubly pleased. Their arrival might also stop Brandon and Ali from fighting.

"Hey." Tyler smiled broadly. "So what are we doing?"

Brandon didn't smile. "Apparently, we're going shopping. Yeah, it seems our reporter here is in need of some retail therapy, or something like that."

Now Ali glared, but Tyler hadn't noticed the

fight. "Sounds good to me—unless you want things to get really smelly around here."

"Really smelly! Really smelly! This is supposed to be a freaking revolution, and you're worried about body odor? Did Lenin put storming the Winter Palace on hold because they'd run out of deodorant? Did Mao halt the Long March because the bath salts hadn't arrived?"

Finally realizing Brandon was having a bad morning, which meant everyone else was supposed to have one too, Tyler's smile faded. "I don't know. Did they even have deodorant back then? And didn't Mao say he washed himself in his women?"

"What? Jesus Christ, I don't believe I'm hearing this! Okay, fine! Sorry, guys. Social justice is gonna have to wait. First, we gotta run down the store for some personal hygiene products."

"Lighten up, man. Nothing will destroy you faster on television than a display of pettiness."

Before Brandon could mix it up with Ross too, Devon decided she'd heard enough. "Can we go now? Because I'm bored, and if I'm bored, Auntie is probably bored too, and you don't want to make Auntie bored, do you?"

No, they didn't. All four of them looked at her and Auntie, suddenly with nothing to say.

"Good, because I want something to eat, and I

want a new dress, and I might want some other stuff as well. I won't know until we get there."

"Of course, sweetie." Ali grinned again. "Uncle Che will buy you whatever you want."

"Stop calling me that. I—"

"You gotta be kidding!" said a voice to the rear of Devon's flock.

Unnoticed by anyone else, a big, black SUV had slid into the parking lot. Four men had stepped out, all wearing black suits, black ties, and black sunglasses. Three of them now stood in a widely spaced line in front of the SUV, while the fourth walked forward. Her flock parted before him to give Devon a clearer view. He looked an awful lot like Melissa, so he probably worked for the bad god CIA too.

Stopping a few yards distant, he paused a moment to take them all in. "My, don't we all look like happy campers. Well, as much as I hate to be the bearer of bad tidings, from now on it gets worse. My name is Agent Richards, and my associates and I are here to explain the current state of play, sort of like it's the fourth quarter, the clock is ticking down, and somebody is sorely in need of a Hail Mary. Before we begin, though, can I just say how great it is to find you all here together in one place? Really, it makes our job so much easier."

"Is that so?" Brandon stepped forward, almost

straining at the leash because here was someone else he could pick a fight with. "Well, you'll excuse me for being stupid, but it seems to me you're the ones in need of a Hail Mary. And exactly who the hell are you, anyway? FBI, Homeland Security, or some other agency we've never even heard of?"

Agent Richards smiled indulgently. "Stupid? No, you're not stupid. Misguided, delusional, incapable of figuring out the consequences of what you're doing, perhaps, but not stupid. As to what agency we work for, you can call us the reality police, if you like. So which part of reality would you like me to explain to you first?"

"How about the part where you're going to stop us? Yeah, I think I'd like to hear that first of all."

"Oh, we know we can't stop you. Not yet, anyway. Yesterday's little incident demonstrated that. We can contain you, though. Think of it like this: you're a virus working its way through the country. We're the immune system. We might not have figured out how to neutralize you yet, but we sure as hell can quarantine you. So feel free. Go in any direction you want. Whichever way you go, you'll find no one you can infect. Go into Baker City, if you don't believe me. It's empty. We evacuated it last night while you were sleeping. We're ready to do that anywhere you go, even in a major city, if you get that far. No one else is going to join your little revolution. No one else is even going to know about it."

That brought Ali forward. "They will when my reports are broadcast."

"Yes, you'll be the reporter. The people you work for were more than happy to cooperate when we explained to them the consequences of not doing so. No more of your reports will ever be broadcast."

"What? You can't do that! What about the First Amendment and freedom of the press?"

"We can do whatever we want, so long as no one ever finds out about it. So there it is. You're now living in a bubble. No one and nothing gets out. No one and nothing gets in." Agent Richards pointed at Auntie. "And when we finally figure out how to deal with that, it'll all be over. Or you could all choose to be reasonable. Yesterday, you were told that if you all went home like good children, there would be no comeback. Of course, the person who made you that offer, and everyone with her, disappeared. That's right. We know about that. We've watched the body cam recordings, right up to the point where the last one went dark. That makes things a little more complicated. So we were thinking of a little vacation, perhaps, somewhere nice and quiet. There won't be any hard time. We know you've been misled. This isn't about punishment. This is about growing up and being an adult. All you have to do is agree to come with us now, and a few years down the road it'll be like nothing ever happened."

The same people as yesterday thought about it, exchanging concerned glances but not quite ready yet to walk. Others were more determined. One of them called out, "Oh yeah? So what's Gitmo like this time of year?"

"Yeah," said another. "I don't look good in orange."

Some of them started to laugh, Brandon included, but not Ali. For her, something a lot more serious was going on here. After their night together, Devon's trust in Ali had grown a lot. If she was unhappy, then Devon probably ought to be too. Auntie certainly was. That familiar chill was already beginning to creep through her. As if he could feel it too, Agent Richards's smile froze. "That's your answer then, is it? Okay. Let us know when you change your minds, but make sure you do so before anything happens that you won't be forgiven for."

No, it wasn't, or at least it wasn't Devon's answer. Once again, no one had bothered to ask her, and that was becoming just a little bit annoying. Tugging on Auntie's hand, she led her to stand a few steps forward of Brandon. Agent Richards and his three men watched, all of them unmoving. Devon didn't know what a body cam was, but if they were telling the truth about knowing what happened to Melissa, they were either very, very brave or very, very stupid. Either way, Agent Richards was behaving far too much like the kid who thought he knew everything.

"Devon?"

Ali was almost alone in never having seen what Auntie could do, if Agent Richards was telling the truth.

Whatever she was concerned about, then, Devon ignored her, saying to Agent Richards, "Hi. My name's Devon, and I want to see the president."

"Well, hello." He smiled broadly again, although it seemed to Devon not really honestly. "We've been looking forward to meeting you, and Auntie too. She's your guardian, right? She looks after you?" Devon nodded in answer to both questions. "So tell me, Devon. What did Auntie do to your parents, because we don't seem to be able to find them either?"

"They're with God, but that's okay because they're happy now. I want to make everyone happy. That's why I want to see the president."

"Of course you do. Who wouldn't want that? But you must understand the president is a very busy man. He can't see just anyone, no matter how much they might want to see him."

"Okay." Devon didn't believe him. He was

just saying something he thought would keep her quiet, like grown-ups did when they weren't really interested in what kids wanted. He needed a lesson in how nobody liked a know-it-all. With a nod of understanding, she looked up at Auntie and pointed at the big, black SUV. "Make that disappear."

A blue ball flew and the SUV crunched and scrunched and squealed up into nothingness.

"Oh my god. Oh shit!"

Stunned into disbelief, Ali stood wide-eyed with a hand raised to her mouth. For all that Agent Richards claimed to know what had happened to Melissa, he and his three men all stared at the spot where their SUV had been as well. Agent Richards even went so far as to take his sunglasses off. None of them looked quite so clever anymore.

"I want to talk to the president. I can come to Washington, if he likes, or he can come see me."

"Er ... okay. We'll, er ... we'll tell him. Yeah, that's what we'll do. So. We know where to find you, so ... um ... that won't be a problem."

"Good. You can go now."

Agent Richards bumbled some more, not quite managing to say anything as he looked to the other three for some kind of support. They were all just as confused as he was. Since none of them showed any sign of going anywhere, Devon told them again,

"You can go now."

Sheepishly, they turned and walked away, plodding from the parking lot like noisy boys who'd just been told to go find something useful to do. Not until they were out on the street did they begin to liven up, throwing their hands about and shaking their heads, clearly arguing with each other—probably about whose fault it all was. Well, someone was going to have to take the blame when the president asked what had happened to their SUV. They would probably say it was all her fault, but Devon didn't care. She heard the murmurings behind her and turned to face them all.

Ali spoke up. "What did you just do?"

"Nothing. Now, are we going into town or not? Because I still want a new dress, a pretty one, the kind a princess ought to wear."

Brandon's mood suddenly brightened. "Whatever you want, sweetheart. One dress fit for a princess coming up, and anything else you want too. All you gotta do is say the word."

Ali, on the other hand, came over all snarky again. "Well, look at you. Your pet killer alien robot destroys an SUV, and all of a sudden you don't mind paying for everything."

"Pay for everything? You heard the man. Baker City is empty. So long as they didn't clean out all the stores and the gas stations, we can just take what we want. So come on, everybody, on the bus. It's everything you can grab day, courtesy of Uncle Sam."

A few minutes later, on the other side of the highway, they drove slowly along Campbell Street, at first through blocks of housing. Agent Richards hadn't lied. Baker City was deserted, a ghost town. All that was missing was tumbleweed rolling by and some broken doors creaking eerily in the wind. Beyond a small park were more businesses, including a supermarket. They pulled into its parking lot, and everyone got out.

Brandon confidently took command again. "Okay. Everyone go find what you need. The law isn't going to bother us, because there isn't any. We're taking this store and everything in it into common ownership."

Some cheers followed; others were more reserved. All of them fell silent when they came to the entrance, which was firmly locked.

"Not a problem, people. We'll just break our way in."

Picking up a trashcan, Brandon threw it at one of the windows. As it bounced off without even leaving a mark, Ali smirked hugely.

"Way to go, genius. The glorious revolution defeated by a plate of glass."

"So? If you got a better suggestion, I'm all ears."

They were about to start arguing again, and Devon sighed. These grown-ups really were completely useless. While they stood around utterly failing to figure it out, she turned to Auntie, not even needing to say it as she pointed at the doors.

Auntie fired a blue bolt, and the doors folded up into themselves like an old cardboard box, their glass cracking and splintering and crackling until not even a single shard was left behind. Ali smirked some more. Brandon fumed. Everyone else rushed for the entrance like it was Santa's grotto and all his little helpers were on lunch break.

Behind them, when it was safe to do so, Ali led Devon inside. Auntie stayed outside. She didn't need a new dress, or anything else, for that matter. First, they went to the kids' clothing section, where Devon found a pale blue princess dress, complete with tiara and a little wand. Once she'd dressed in that, with matching shoes, Ali insisted they choose some other clothes as well. Then she insisted they find soap and toothpaste and toothbrushes and a whole lot of other things like that. It was boring, but as Ali explained, "Even princesses have to brush their teeth, sweetheart, otherwise, they might end up not having any, and no prince is going to want to kiss a princess who doesn't have any teeth."

"That doesn't sound very fair. What if the prince

doesn't have any teeth? Would I still have to kiss him and marry him, even though I brushed my teeth and he didn't?"

"No. Of course not. You don't have to do anything you don't want to do."

"Well, I know that. Not while Auntie's here, anyway. But sometimes princesses are made to do things they don't want to do, like marry a prince they don't like."

"Yes, but that's only in fairy tales. A lot of us have fought long and hard to make sure things like that don't happen anymore."

"Okay then. I'll brush my teeth, but the prince had better be nice."

About an hour later, they left the supermarket with Ali's arms overflowing with clothes and bags filled with this and that. So were everyone else's. They'd liberated an awful lot of stuff, and Brandon was grinning from ear to ear.

Devon wasn't quite so happy. Since she could have anything she wanted, there was another thing, something someone else really should've thought of by now. "I don't think a princess should be riding in the back of a truck. It's just not right, that's all. A princess would ride in a big coach with white horses and footmen to help her in and out, like Cinderella."

"Of course, sweetheart, but I don't think we're

going to find a coach and horses around here."

Ali was trying not to disappoint, but as Devon pointed out, "Well, you could try. I mean, you haven't even looked yet."

"Okay." Brandon exchanged a look with Ali. For once, they seemed to agree about something. "Everybody, let's go find something for Devon to ride in, then."

"Great!" someone said as they all fanned out. "This revolution is being run by a princess. All we need now is a white knight and a dragon. Make that a privileged white knight oppressing a dragon."

Brandon was quick to reply. "Just can it, okay. Auntie gets what Auntie wants, and if Auntie wants to be a princess, Auntie gets to be a princess."

He sounded a little confused. Auntie wasn't a princess. Devon was, but even Ali didn't quite get it. Once they were alone together, she crouched down in front of Devon with a terribly serious look on her face. "Sweetie, you do understand, don't you? Being a princess is only make-believe."

"Why? If I want to be a princess and have all the pretty things princesses have, why can't I?"

"Well, nobody minds you pretending to be a princess. I used to pretend I was a princess when I was your age, but it was only pretending. Besides, good princesses don't simply demand things. They ask politely because then people will be happy to help them. I thought you wanted to be a good princess so you could make the world a nicer place."

Devon had to think about that one. She looked down at the ground, because, once again, Ali had made her feel slightly guilty. "Yes ... I do ... but when I'm nice, no one listens to me. Jesus was nice, and lots of people didn't listen to him either. They nailed him to a cross instead."

Ali smiled patiently. "Oh, sweetie. Lots of people listened to Jesus, not right away perhaps, but then that's why he let them kill him, so that people would listen to him after he was gone, like people are still listening to him now."

"Not all of them. There are still lots of people doing bad things."

"Yes, but that's because those people are still not listening. People have to choose to listen, sweetheart. You can't force them to. You can't—"

"Why not? If people can choose to do bad things, why can't I choose to stop them? If people can choose not to listen, why can't I choose to make them? God gave Auntie to me to help him make the world a nicer place. If they won't listen to me, they will listen to Auntie or Auntie will send them to God, and he'll make them do detention or something."

"No, Devon, it's not like that at all. You must

promise me that you won't let Auntie send any people to God. He wants us to be nice to each other, for sure, but that doesn't mean he wants you to make all the bad people disappear. He—"

"Then why did he give me Auntie? Why did God answer me when I asked him for help? And why did he make Auntie able to send people to him? You know what I think? I think you're not listening either."

"Devon, God didn't—"

"No! I think you better start listening or maybe Auntie will get mad with you!"

CHAPTER NINE

Devon sat on the tailgate of the truck. Right now she felt a little lonely. Auntie stood quietly nearby, but Ali had walked away in a sulk. Making people be nice to each other wasn't so good if it made her the kid no one wanted to talk to. Fortunately, the feeling didn't last long. All her followers, who'd gone out to find her a carriage fit for a princess, began to return. They came in twos and threes, all of them empty-handed. That wasn't so good, but just when it seemed she might have to go without, a canary-colored school bus appeared. It was one of those small ones, short and boxy but with big windows on its sides. Turning into the parking lot, it squeaked to a halt not far from her, and out jumped Tyler. "Hey, Devon. Come see what we found for you."

"Okay."

She jumped down from the tailgate and hurried on over, almost forgetting to take Auntie by the hand because this morning had suddenly become interesting again. Tyler and three others waited for her by the back of the bus. All of them were smiling but not with really happy smiles. Rather, their smiles said that although they were happy with what they'd done, they wouldn't be really happy until they knew she was happy. Well, she would see about that.

Devon walked round to the back of the bus and saw the rear door already open and some small steps in front of it. Inside, about half the regular seating had been removed. In their place sat two big, leather chairs, roughly bolted to the floor.

"Well?" Tyler was all puppyish again, only without the wagging tail. "Do you like it? It took us, like, forever to find everything and put it all together. So what do you think?"

It was nothing like a grand coach pulled by white horses with some footmen and all, but never mind. If she pretended hard enough, it would be. Yellow was almost gold and those big chairs were almost thrones. She sat in one of them, sinking slightly into the firmness beneath her. She had to raise her arms to use its rests. From here, she could look out the back of the bus and have everybody look up at her, just like a princess should.

Right now, four hopeful faces looked up at her, all waiting to be told how well they'd done. Well, not yet. Auntie still had to be fitted in. The door certainly looked wide enough, and the chair looked big enough, but there was only one way to be sure. Devon thought-called Auntie to her, and all five of them watched as she squeezed her way through the door and sat in the other chair. Everything was now as it should be.

Devon smiled. "Yes. I'm happy. Thank you."

They were too. Their smiles turned to real happiness as she blessed them with her approval, just as Ali had said she should.

"Now find me something nice to eat."

They rushed away with Tyler leading them into the supermarket. What they might come back with was a mystery, a big surprise that Devon felt sure she'd like—unless, of course, she didn't. While she waited, she looked out the back of the bus upon her little realm. She told Auntie to step down and stand by the open door, like some splendid knight who would make sure she wasn't bothered by any annoying people. Not that anyone was trying to bother her. Almost all her flock was here, sitting around the parking lot eating whatever they'd chosen from inside the supermarket. Ali and Ross sat in the back of their van, having what appeared to be another heated conversation. That left only Brandon and the two who'd gone with him, who'd not yet returned. That would be another surprise to look forward to, and it would have to be a very good one if he wanted to please her.

When Tyler and his three companions returned, all sorts of things filled their arms. Tyler nodded toward each in turn as he offered them up. "So what would you like, Devon? We got milk and cookies. We got soda and candy. We even got some fruit because, well, everybody likes fruit, don't they?"

Sometimes, but only if there was nothing else. Devon liked ice cream, but they hadn't brought any. It was possible there might not be any, or it was possible they simply hadn't tried hard enough to find it. She could send them back, telling them that princesses really oughtn't have to think of things like that for themselves. Then again, Ali was still right. Princesses who wanted everyone else to be nice really ought to be nice themselves.

"Are they chocolate chip cookies?"

"These are." Tyler picked a packet from among the ones in his arm, holding it out to her like it was some fabled treasure many knights had died to win for her.

"Okay then. I'll have milk and cookies. Open them for me, please."

Tyler did so. Then he and his three companions settled down on the other side of the door from Auntie with their own food. Devon munched on a cookie, enjoying its crumbliness and the meltiness of its bits of chocolate, all the while looking out over her domain. Nothing much had changed, except for Ali and Ross. No longer arguing—if that's what they'd been doing—now they were fussing over their equipment as if they meant to start recording. Quite what there was to record, Devon couldn't see, until a large, boxy van appeared, the kind delivery drivers used. It pulled up in the parking lot, and Brandon and his two guys jumped out of it. They seemed quite pleased with themselves until they saw Devon sitting in the back of the school bus. Their smiles instantly wilted, Brandon's in particular. Poor Brandon. He was trying so hard to please and failing so terribly at it.

As he stood sullenly witnessing how he'd been upstaged again, Ali hurried over to talk to him. They would bicker. Devon knew they would because that's what they always did. For a few moments, it looked as though she might be right, with both of them squaring off like two dogs who weren't quite sure whether they liked each other or not yet. Then they talked, with several pointed glances in Devon's direction. As much as she would've loved to know what they were saying, there was no way to do that. Then she didn't need to, because as soon as they were done, Brandon came over to talk to her.

"Hey. I see someone found you what you wanted. I wasn't quite so successful, but I tried, right? And we can still put it to good use, don't you think?"

Devon didn't answer. She had learned from watching her parents that sometimes saying nothing was enough to keep other people talking. That was strange, but then she was just a kid, and kids didn't know things like that. They were probably afraid of the silence. It was something they had to fill, and now Brandon had to fill this one.

"So, Devon, or should I say Princess Devon? Is everything the way you want it, or is there something else you'd like? You know you only have to tell me and I'll get it for you, don't you?"

"No."

"No what? There's nothing else you want, or you don't know that I only want to help? Look, Devon, I know I've made some mistakes, and I'm sorry for that, but I've never tried to hurt you or put you in danger, have I? I just want to make the world a nicer place, like you do."

"Is that why you wanted me to make Melissa disappear?"

"Yes, and I was right, wasn't I? She wanted to

take Auntie away from you. They all did, but Auntie wouldn't let them because she knew. They still want to take her away—"

"But so do you. That's why you asked me all those questions yesterday. You want to know how to make Auntie do what you want, so then you won't need me."

"No. No, of course not. My god, Devon, is that what you think I've been trying to do? God gave Auntie to you. I know that. I couldn't take her away from you even if I wanted to. If anything, I want to be like Auntie. That's why I was asking all those questions, so that I could help you like she does."

Devon was silent again, but this time it wasn't to make Brandon feel uncomfortable. He sounded like he was being honest, but then he always did. Or maybe she was just being unkind, which was something princesses shouldn't do. After all, if he was truly nasty, like a Nazi or someone who worked for the bad god CIA, he wouldn't be here at all. Devon decided she would believe him, for now.

"Okay then. So where are we going next?"

"Anywhere that gets us closer to Washington. You still want to meet the president, right? Well, if he won't come to us, we'll just have to keep right on going to him."

"Okay, but I want Tyler and his friends on the

bus with me."

"You got it."

Brandon walked away, looking much happier than he had when he came. Ali was waiting for him, but they barely exchanged a dozen words before he waved her away. He had more important things to do, like get the convoy moving, than listen to whatever she wanted to talk about. Again, Devon wondered what that might be. She would have to find out at some point, if only to satisfy her curiosity. For now, she munched on another cookie, because that was far more interesting.

Half an hour later, having found a gas station and filled their tanks, the convoy set out eastward and then south on the highway. The scenery was boring, a long and mostly straight road running through brown hills covered in scrub, and everyone was silent. Devon munched her way through some more cookies. If it was going to be like this all the way to Washington, then she wanted some videos to watch like she could in the back seat of her parents' car. Somebody ought to be trying to keep her entertained, or at the very least just saying something.

At last Tyler did. "I guess Agent Richards wasn't joking. We're all alone out here."

"Yeah," one of his companions said. "So do you really think they can evacuate every large town we come to, or was that all just talk? I mean, were they just trying to make us give up, or can they actually do that?"

Tyler shrugged. "Dunno. The next big place through these mountains is Boise. We'll find out when we get there, I guess."

"So we're good for now, but what happens if we get to Boise and they try to stop us again?"

"They won't, and even if they do, Auntie won't let them. Isn't that right, Devon? Auntie won't let the bad people stop us, will she?"

"Uh-uh." As bored with cookies as she was with this landscape, Devon left her big chair to join Tyler and his friends. "I've never been out of California before, except when we go to our lake, of course. So is everywhere going to be like this?"

"No, sweetheart. Once we get through the mountains, everything will be green for as far as you can see."

The blonde girl sitting next to her had a cascade of long hair flowing over the shoulders of her leather jacket. She wore jeans and boots, a lot of bangles and necklaces, and had a pretty smile and hazel eyes. Devon thought she might like her, but still, she said, "I don't know you."

"Well, okay. A little blunt, perhaps, but I'm Laura. These two are James and Madison, and Tyler, of course, you already know."

James and Madison were almost a pair. Dressed much like Laura, they both had short brown hair and round faces. Maybe they were brother and sister, or even twins.

"So do you all go to school together?"

"That's right," Madison said. "We share classes—really hard stuff, y'know."

"Yes. My school makes us do really hard stuff too, like math. I don't like math. I like making things."

"Yeah," said Laura. "So what things do you like making, Devon?"

"Oh, I like making pretty things like butterflies and paintings where everyone is happy. I think everyone should be happy, don't you?"

"Well, of course," said Madison. "Everyone should be happy."

"So why isn't Brandon happy, then?"

"Brandon?" Tyler glanced back at them from the driver's seat. "Well, Brandon's complicated."

"Complicated!" said James. "Seems like a bit of a dick to me."

"Oh, he's not that bad. He's, well, he can be pretty intense, I'll give you that, but he means well."

James snorted. "Intense! That's one way of putting it. Don't get me wrong. I'm all for taking down corrupt politicians and corporations, but that

130

guy just wants to start a fight, with anybody. I'm not sure he even needs a reason."

"Like I said, he can be pretty intense, but that doesn't make him a bad person. As for starting a fight, well, you can't win one if you don't start one, can you? And what's the alternative? Just sit there and let them get away with it? Sometimes you just gotta stand up and say no."

"If you say so, but one day he's going to pick the wrong fight. That's all I'm saying."

Tyler laughed. "We're going to Washington to confront the president, and you're worried about picking the wrong fight? Shit, dude. You need to start paying attention. As for Brandon, don't worry about it. I met him a couple of years ago at a demo. He knows an awful lotta stuff, y'know, about how the system works and how it's all set up to screw us over. He showed me what books to read, what talks to go to. I learned a lot. If only everybody else in this country would wake up to the truth, we wouldn't even need to be doing this."

"Right," said Laura. "So he showed you all that, but he never told you he had a trust fund."

"Yeah, well, so what? Maybe it's because he's got a trust fund that he found out all that stuff to begin with. Besides, he doesn't like to talk about himself that much. You gotta respect that, right?"

Devon saw it rather differently. "I don't like him. I think he wants Auntie for himself."

Tyler glanced at her in the rearview mirror. "Now why would you think that, Devon? We all know Auntie is yours. Besides, he doesn't want to take things away from people. He just wants to make sure everyone gets a fair share, is all."

"Really?" said James. "Because I think what she just said might be the truest thing that's been said here."

"Anyway," said Madison. "We're all here together. So long as we all want the same thing, what does it matter?"

"It matters a lot," said Devon. "Auntie is mine."

Everyone fell silent after that, a sort of mildly embarrassed, best-say-nothing kind of silence. It was only for a little while, though. Soon enough they were talking again, the kind of harmless chitchat that couldn't offend anyone. It filled the next two hours or so until they came to a junction outside Caldwell. There, four people stood by the side of the highway frantically waving, like maybe there'd been a crash up ahead or something.

"What the hell?" Tyler sounded unsure.

James didn't. "No, Brandon, don't stop. No ... Brandon! Oh for ..."

With his truck in the lead, Brandon brought the convoy to a halt. Oh well. Even if he had been able to hear Tyler and James, he probably wouldn't have listened. He and his guy stepped out, and Tyler was quick to join them. Not wanting to be left out, Devon followed on behind, bringing Auntie with her. Close up, she saw these four people were young. They were also a bit grungy, disheveled, and hairy, a lot like the street people her parents had always told her to stay away from. It was strange that some of them should be out here, because usually, they stayed in the city. More importantly, though, street people could become really mad really quickly, and Brandon was quite possibly spoiling for another fight.

One of them approached, leaving the others to hold back a little. "Sup, guys. My name's Jake. We heard about you and thought we might join up."

"Really? Because they told us no one would be allowed to come near us."

Brandon was being good, for a change, or maybe he was holding back for another reason. Jake seemed nice enough, but then it was too early to be sure. Whatever Brandon might be thinking, Devon let him be in charge some more.

"They told us that too. Some bullshit story about a chemical spill. We knew it was you, so we slipped past them while they weren't looking."

Ali and Ross had joined them, and Ross recorded it all, while Ali picked holes. "How did you know it was us? They buried the story, didn't they? And who is it you slipped past? Do they have troops out there?"

"Whoa. Too many questions. Yeah, they got troops out there. They got troops in all the big cities too, or at least National Guard. It's, like, crazy nuts, y'know. People watched your report, and they're out on the streets. They're calling themselves Auntie's Army and sticking it to the fascists wherever they can find them. Well, not the sheeple. They're all still sat there in front of their TVs, like, nothing to see here, guys. Go to sleep. Go to sleep. For the rest of us, somebody uploaded your report to the internet. It's gone viral, like, globally. Half the planet must have watched it by now."

"Wow." Tyler seemed impressed, for a moment anyway. "What? That's good, isn't it? We got people rising up and fighting back at last."

"Maybe." Brandon wasn't nearly so impressed. "So exactly how did you find us? They're not letting anyone in or out, right, and they're not letting anyone know where we are. So how did you know we'd be here?"

"We followed your trail, dude, from the fake news in Tacoma through that light aircraft crash—yeah, like that happened, right?—to the TV broadcast in Yakima and then the fake spill in Baker City. We figured out you must be on I-84 and just waited for you to show up. Hey, we ain't stooges. We want to join up with you. Really, we can help."

"Oh yeah?" Devon looked up at Brandon. He was starting to get antsy. "And how exactly you gonna do that?"

Jake gestured toward his three companions, who were all standing there gawking at Auntie. "You haven't uploaded anything since Yakima, right? So we got to thinking maybe they closed you down. You tried your phones today? No signal, right? Is that because there's no coverage out here or is it because they shut the system down? Whatever. They can't shut the entire planet down. What you need is access, and we can help you with that. You got a van full of equipment, right? Well, we got code. Seriously. We can connect you to a satellite so you can talk to the entire planet if you want to. Think about it, dude. Billions of people watching you live. It'll be the biggest thing ever."

Brandon continued to look unconvinced. "You're hackers? All the way out here in the middle of nowhere."

Jake seemed a little hurt by that. "Well, yeah. Hey, dude, we got electricity and running water and all that stuff, just like in the big cities, y'know."

Ali didn't look too convinced either. "You're going to hack us into a satellite. Well, I don't know a whole lot about that, but it seems to me those things have got to be pretty secure."

Reaching into a pocket, Jake pulled out a thumb drive. "Trust us, baby, and we'll amaze you. And if you should happen to need any nuclear weapons along the way, we'll hack you into North Korea's defense computers as well."

CHAPTER
TEN

Tyler wasn't at all happy with that. "Are you for real? We don't want to destroy the world. We want to make it a nicer place."

"Okay, okay. No need to sweat it, dude. I'm just saying, that's all. Y'know, just in case you need it."

Ali wasn't too impressed either. "Good to know, but I think we'll leave the North Koreans out of it, if it's all the same to you. Now about this uplink; if we record something, you can put it out there for the whole world to see. That's what you're saying, right?"

Jake grinned broadly, holding up the thumb drive and twiddling it before her. "That's about the size of it. It's all right here, like a digital open sesame."

"Great. Ross."

While Ross led Jake and the others away to the van, Ali looked toward Brandon. He'd fallen strangely silent, as if not picking a fight had completely thrown his day. Instead, misty-eyed, he gazed off to the far horizon.

"You better not be thinking what I think you're thinking," Ali said. "We are not threatening our own country with someone else's nuclear weapons."

Her words jerked him back. "What? What kind of person do you think I am? Of course we're not doing that. Why would we need to, anyway? We got Auntie. If what they said is true, we're already winning, and we've barely even started."

"If what they say is true, and if you consider civil unrest winning."

He grinned. "Oh, I agree. How about that for unheard of? So what we do now is the last thing they expect us to do. Devon can appeal for calm. You record it, then upload it for the whole world to see, and suddenly we're the good guys."

She grinned. "How about *that* for unheard of? You, a peacemaker. I wouldn't have thought that was in your playbook."

"Everything's in my playbook if it throws the opposition off-balance, baby."

"Well, aren't you just the regular Sun Tzu."

"I've read him, and Machiavelli too. Everything's fair in love and war, and only the winners get to write history. Now, if you'll excuse me, I got a speech to write for Devon."

"*We* got a speech to write for Devon."

Pretty much all of what Brandon and Ali were saying was meaningless to Devon, but she understood that last bit well enough. "I'm making a speech?"

Ali smiled down at her. "Yes, sweetheart. You're going to talk into the camera, and the whole world will see it."

Devon nodded. Speaking into a camera was easy enough. That was something else God should have thought of when he sent Jesus to tell the world to be nice to each other.

Half an hour later, in the middle of the empty highway, Devon stood at the back door of the bus in her blue princess dress, with her tiara set firmly upon her head, her wand grasped in one hand, and the speech they'd written for her in the other. Auntie stood to her right next to the steps, and Brandon stood to her left. Everyone else formed a circle around them, except Ross and Ali, who stood on the other side of it. Ali was now firmly in charge.

"Okay. We'll do a run-through first. So, Devon, when you're ready, just read out loud to us, yes?"

Devon held up the speech, took a deep breath, and, as carefully as she could, began to read. "Hi. My name is Devon. These are all my friends, and we want to live in a world where everyone can have what they need. We want to live in a world where everyone can be whatever they want to be, without poverty, ex … exploit …"

Devon stopped. There were far too many big words she couldn't say or understand. She looked up at all those faces looking back at her. What they thought of them, she couldn't tell, but she knew what she thought. "This speech is silly. I just want everyone to be nice to each other. And my name isn't Devon. It's Princess Devon."

Ali hurried over, looking all concerned, probably because this was really, really important, and she wanted Devon to get it right. "No, sweetie. I know it's nice being a princess, but this is America and some people might get angry if they thought a princess was telling them what to do."

"Why? I thought you said the whole world would see. They have princesses in England, and everybody loves them, don't they?"

"Well, yes, and maybe one day you'll get to go to England, and everybody there will love you too. But, you see, England isn't the whole world. It's just one small part of it. There are lots and lots of other people in the world and they—"

"Don't like princesses? Why? Are they all Nazis?"

Ali sighed. "Yeah, we're gonna have to sit down and have a serious talk about this whole Nazi thing, aren't we? In the meantime, Devon, just don't call yourself a princess, okay? And if you don't want to read the speech, that's okay too. Just tell everyone what it is you want to do. And don't say anything about making people disappear either. You'll just scare them, and you don't want to do that, do you?"

"Except for the—"

"No! No Nazis, okay? Just don't even mention them."

Devon looked down at her. Quite why Ali didn't want her to even mention the bad people, she didn't know. Making the bad people be nice or answer to God for it was the whole point, after all. Oh well. Ali was a reporter. She spoke into the camera all the time, so Devon could only trust she had a good reason for it.

"Okay."

"Great!"

Ali walked away, spreading her hands and shaking her head as she glanced at Brandon. Once more at Ross's side, she exchanged a few words with him, and then they were ready. "Okay, sweetie. In your own time."

Devon wasn't ready at all. With all those faces looking at her, she suddenly wasn't sure what to say. It ought to have been easy, but for Ali telling her all the things she shouldn't say. That was why grown-ups always made things so difficult and complicated, because they could never quite seem to just say what they meant. Well, it was up to her now, and all those faces were waiting for her to say something, so she'd better get on with it.

"Hello. My name is ... Devon. I'm seven, and I think everyone should be nice to each other. So does God, even though you were all horrible to Jesus. This is Auntie. God gave her to me and, well, Auntie is helping me. All these other people are helping me too. You can help me as well if you like. Then we can all make the ..." Devon paused. She wasn't allowed to say Nazis, so she looked again at the speech Brandon had given her, but all those big words still meant nothing to her. It didn't really matter. She knew what she wanted to say. "Then we can all live in a world where everyone can be whatever they want and have whatever they want. No one should be poor because bad people make silly laws and then take everything for themselves. Everyone should be kind to everyone else, and to all the animals and the plants and the fishes in the sea. Everyone should have somewhere to live too, and not be forced to sleep in tents on the street, like all those people in San Francisco. Everyone should just stop being nasty, and selfish, and stop bullying other people, and, well, everything like that. I think we should because God wants us to. That's all."

Devon fell silent. For a few moments, everyone around her was silent too. They must be thinking she'd got it all wrong, like she'd said something she shouldn't have, and now they were all really, really mad at her. But no, because suddenly everyone broke out into applause, cheering and whooping and shouting about how wonderful it had been. She smiled, swelling with happiness because she hadn't messed it up at all.

Even Ali smiled as she hurried back. "That was beautiful, Devon. You said all the right things and didn't offend anyone."

"You think?" Of course, Brandon had to find fault. "I'm not so sure about all that God stuff."

Ali turned a harsh gaze upon him. "Don't, all right? You may not believe it, but she does and so do a lot of other people out there. You want your little revolution to succeed, don't you? So you tell them what they already believe, not what you think they should believe."

Almost impressed, but not really, or so it seemed to Devon, Brandon grinned. "Wow! I think you must've been doing some reading too. Or is that all just some PR gobbledygook you just came out with?"

"What if it is? That's why I'm here, isn't it? That and looking out for her."

"So not because you believe, then."

"Believe what? That you're going to save the world? Do me a favor!"

Devon had heard enough. "Stop it! You're always fighting with each other. I don't like it."

"Of course, honey. I'm sorry. But we're not really fighting, y'know. We're just trying to figure what the best thing to do is, and sometimes that means we argue about it. Isn't that right, Brandon?" Since he didn't answer immediately, Ali repeated rather more firmly, "Isn't that right, Brandon?"

"Yeah. Of course. Whatever you say."

Brandon scowled as if he'd just been told to play nice with his sister, but Ali smiled. "That's right. Whatever I say. So we'll clean it up a little, maybe film some short interviews with some of the others to go along with it, and then our hacker friends can put it up there for the entire world to see. You happy with that, Devon?"

Devon nodded. It all sounded good to her. Not so much to Brandon. Every day, it seemed, there was something new he didn't like, apart from Ali of course, who he didn't like all the time. He watched her walk away, staring sourly at her back.

His words were something else Devon found hard to understand. "Don't you like God?"

"I ... wouldn't ... necessarily say that. I just think ... maybe ... God could've done a better job, that's all."

"Yes. God could've given Jesus an Auntie of his own and a ... PR guru, but he didn't. So now I'm helping him make it right. You're not mad at that, are you?"

"No, of course not. I just—"

"Good. Can we go now, then, because I'm bored?"

In fact, another hour passed before they moved on, but that was all right because Tyler and his friends made it their job to keep Devon entertained. It was almost midday by the time they came to Boise. Thick trees, fencing, and walls hid the highways from barely glimpsed suburbs. The only signs of life were people in twos and threes who waved to them from bridges as they passed beneath.

That puzzled Tyler a little. "Where are they all coming from? I thought those agents said no one was being let in or out."

Laura, who sat next to him up front, replied with a shrug. "Dunno. Maybe they were just lying to us when they said they could evacuate whole towns before we got there. Or maybe these people hid out in their basements."

The highway that took them toward the center of town was more open with parking lots and businesses and suchlike to either side. Up ahead distant mountains stood, hazy beneath a clear sky.

As they rolled toward them, other vehicles began to join the rear of the convoy. By the time they came off onto West Fairview Avenue, the convoy had almost doubled in size. Main Street followed, now with taller buildings, so that Boise began to feel like a city. At last, they came to a pub, the road in front of it blocked by a crowd. They cheered, and more people poured out of the pub, all of them with glasses or bottles in hand.

That set Tyler worrying about something else. "So much for evacuation. Everyone just decided to party instead?"

"Well, why not? At least we know somebody's pleased to see us."

Laura's words were met with laughter until they saw Brandon get out of his truck.

As some of his guys hurried up to back him up, Tyler's misgivings grew. "Oh great. Trust fund boy's gonna talk to the common man. This should be fun."

They all got out, joining all the others from the bus and the new recruits behind it. Ali and Ross stood nearby recording it all, with Jake and his friends behind them. For some reason, they looked rather sorry for themselves. Facing them in front of the pub, stood the residents of Boise, a crowd as happy as they were noisy. To Devon they seemed overly happy, a lot like the elf people around the fire in the woods had been. She hadn't quite understood why then, and she didn't quite understand why now either.

Tyler did, though. "You know who these people are, don't you? They're the ones who gave the authorities the finger, and if you ask me, they're hammered. This could go south real fast."

"What's the finger?" Devon looked up at Tyler, expecting a reply, but no one was listening. They were all too busy watching Brandon climb onto the back of his truck. With a big smile he raised his hands, meaning to quiet the Boise crowd down. "Friends. Friends, listen. We—"

"Stop whistling, son," cried someone at the back of the crowd, none of whom seemed to want to quiet down. "We ain't interested in you. We're interested in that."

"Yeah," said another. "What is that? A mascot or something?"

"So where's the team?" said a third.

"To hell with the team," shouted a fourth. "Where are the cheerleaders, boy? C'mon, show us the girls."

Brandon's smile disappeared. "We're not a football team." Sounding terribly serious and ever so slightly offended, he continued, "Haven't you people seen our video? We're a people's army marching on Washington to—"

"A people's army?" cried another voice. "You look

like a bunch of school kids to me, except for you. You look like one of those West Coast liberals with your head stuffed full of commie bullshit and your bank account stuffed full of money. How about you show us some of that equality you people like to preach about by buying us all a drink, huh?"

"Really? Is that all you care about? Getting drunk while the politicians and bankers rob you blind?"

"Hey, kid," said someone else. "If anyone's doing any thieving around here, it's me, unless the goddamn cops get in the way of course."

The Boise crowd roared with laughter. They were all having lots of fun, which was good. Devon might have been having fun with them but for the chill she was beginning to feel from Auntie. Though quietly neutral for the whole morning, she was now unhappy. It must be all the noisiness that unsettled her, unless it was something Devon couldn't see, like another drone. Whatever it was, Devon set herself to willing that chilliness away, only half listening as Brandon tried again to win the Boise crowd over.

"Well, yeah, the cops as well, giving you a hard time while you're just trying to get by. We want to change all that. We want to—"

"You wanna what?" said the last person to speak. "You wanna make thievery legal?"

"Why not? They stole it from us, didn't they?

Why shouldn't we take it back and then—"

"Well, hell, I'm up for that. I could use a new TV and a fridge full of beer. How about the rest of you?"

If their cheers and applause were anything to judge by, the entire Boise crowd was up for it, and Brandon grinned again. As confidently smug as he might be, though, he was the only one. Everyone else in Devon's flock looked like they'd caught Auntie's chill, and none more so than Tyler. Taking a couple of steps forward, he called to Brandon over the noise. "What are you doing, dude?"

"I'm winning them over. Look, they're loving it."

"No, you're not. You're just stoking them up. Can't you see that? These people aren't interested in your revolution. They just want—"

"Oh, quit worrying. I know what I'm doing. All I have to do is explain it to them properly, and they'll understand."

"Brandon—"

But Brandon wasn't listening. Returning to the Boise crowd, he began again. "Listen. Friends ..."

Tyler shook his head, then hurried over to Ali, who was looking just as concerned. After exchanging a few words, they began to usher people back onto the bus and into the other vehicles. As the ones at the back reversed away, Tyler hurried over to Devon. "You and Auntie get back on the bus, okay? The rest of you too, before that idiot starts a riot."

Devon had seen a riot on TV. It was a lot of people being really mad about something. These people weren't mad about anything, not yet, anyway. Of course, Tyler might be right. If Brandon did start a fight, someone would have to put a stop to it before anyone, including Brandon, got hurt. That someone wasn't going to be Tyler.

"No. Everyone is going to be nice to each other. I'm going to make sure they do."

"Devon. Be good and get back on the bus."

"No. You be good if you want, but Auntie and me are staying right here."

By now all the rest of the convoy had reversed back along the street. No one in the Boise crowd seemed to have noticed. They were too busy listening to one of the first voices to have spoken, who was now saying, "That's all well and good, boy, but what I want to know is, who's inside that carnival suit?"

CHAPTER ELEVEN

The speaker stepped out of the crowd. He was big, with a long beard and shaven head. Thick arms stuck out to either side of him, like two logs pushed apart by the boulder of his chest. It bulged inside his black and grubby leather vest, the same as his pants and heavy boots. To Devon, he looked an awful lot like an ogre, except he didn't have green skin, although it was hard to tell what with him being covered all over in tattoos. Green skin or not, ogres weren't nice at all. Even more determined to stay, then, just in case this one tried to eat someone, Devon simply ignored Tyler as he tried one more time.

"Devon! Come on!"

The ogre walked halfway toward the truck, planting himself as if he meant to take root. "Boy, I don't care nothin' 'bout no politicians or bankers.

Yeah, they're all corrupt as hell, but if it wasn't for the corruption, half of us wouldn't have two pennies to rub together. So what're you gonna do? Take away the one means we got of makin' any kind of a livin'? You got somethin' better to offer, or are you just another one of them commies come to tell us how we all ought to be grateful for havin' nothin'?"

"That's what I'm trying to explain to you. We can—"

"Explain to me. You wanna explain somethin' to me; you tell me who's inside that suit."

Tyler placed his hand on Devon's shoulder. "Devon."

Once again, Devon ignored him. She could feel the growing chill from Auntie too, but she ignored that. Watching Brandon stumble over his words was simply too good to miss. "Well … I don't know—"

"You don't know? Boy, I wanna see who's inside that suit. Now you gonna show me or do I gotta look for myself?"

Brandon flicked a glance at Auntie. "Oh, I wouldn't do that, if I were you. Seriously. Don't even think about it."

The ogre smiled. Well, they weren't that smart either. Devon had already confronted Nazis and the bad god CIA. As big and scary as this ogre might be, she was not the least bit scared to confront him too.

"You can't do that," she said. "If you try, Auntie will get mad and then she'll make you disappear."

As if God himself had spoken, every face turned to her. The ogre, like many in the Boise crowd, seemed to notice her for the first time. Silence followed as if none of them quite knew what to do or say. Then someone in the crowd called out, "Whoa! Looks like the little girl's in charge. Whatcha gonna do now, brother?"

Everyone laughed, except for the ogre. He glanced toward them, not amused at all, which only made them laugh all the more. Clearly, ogres also didn't like being laughed at, and this one grew more annoyed by the second. Slowly, with a passing glance at Devon, he turned back to Brandon. "Is that right? The little girl's in charge?"

Brandon didn't answer. He was too busy staring, like the kid who was almost licking his lips because a fight was about to start. That the ogre might choose to rip his head off, just for fun, was something he didn't appear to have realized yet.

Before that could happen, Devon tried to set the ogre straight. "I'm not a little girl. I'm a princess, and you ought to be nice to me."

"You heard her," said another voice in the Boise crowd. "She's royalty."

"Yeah," said a third. "You better be nice to her,

or she'll have that suit arrest you and throw you in a dungeon."

At the same time, Tyler said, "Devon. Don't!"

"Don't what? It's not me who's being a bully. It's him."

"Maybe so. But still. You can't—"

"Oh, shush!"

While Devon dismissed Tyler, the first voice in the crowd called out, "So whatcha gonna do, brother? You gonna kiss her feet or kiss her ass?"

There was more laughter, but not from the ogre. Finished with Brandon, he now eyed up Devon, probably thinking she would make a tasty little morsel, like all that finger food her parents used to pass around at parties.

Certainly, as he crouched down a little with his hands resting on his knees, the look in his eyes was hungry for something. "Hey, little girl. For sure, you're pretty as a princess but, you see, that don't necessarily count for nothin' until you're a whole lot older. Now, I wanna know who's inside that suit, so why don't you be a good little girl and tell me?"

"No. I'm not afraid of any ogre, and neither is Auntie."

To a chorus of oohs, the ogre straightened, his face clouding over. "Now, don't you make me come on over there and tan your hide, missy."

"Yeah, that's telling her," said another voice in

the crowd, followed by, "You do it, man," and, "We don't take no crap from royalty, sweetheart. This here is America!"

Devon waited for them to finish. Ogres were scary, but only if people let them be. If someone stood up to them, they were simply too dumb to do anything but lumber about causing trouble. All they really needed was a good talking to. So, with Tyler still chafing at her shoulder, she would explain it to this one, just once. If he chose not to listen, well, that would be his fault.

"This is Auntie. She's my gift from God. She does what I tell her to do, and she isn't going to do what you say, because I say no."

The ogre began to glower. "You're trying my patience, kid. I'll ask just one more time. Who's in the suit?"

"Or what? You'll eat me?"

"Well, maybe I will. Or maybe I'll eat him."

He turned toward Brandon.

Whatever Devon might think of him, Brandon belonged to her. She wasn't going to let some ogre eat him. Raising a finger, she said, "Auntie, fire!"

A red ball flew, and the ogre glowed and hissed.

Once he was gone, the stunned silence that followed broke when various voices in the crowd said, "Shit!" and, "Oh my god!" and, "I am outta here!"

Some ran. The rest remained, too shocked to move. Brandon still stood in the back of his truck, now with a huge grin on his face. It didn't matter to Devon, because he'd failed, again. *She* had made them listen. *She* was the center of their attention now, which, of course, was only as it should be.

Behind her, Tyler snapped, "Devon!"

But she ignored him. Walking forward with Auntie at her side, she met their stares with one of her own. "I am Princess Devon, and I order you to follow me."

No one spoke. No one quibbled or complained. Into that silence, Devon continued, "God wants me to make everyone be nice to each other. Making fun of people and laughing at them isn't very nice. It's what little kids do. I think you should all say sorry before Auntie gets mad."

People exchanged glances. Some of them were filled with doubt, others verging on defiant. That wouldn't do at all, so Devon added, "I thought grown-ups were supposed to know better. Isn't that why they're always telling kids what to do? Well, now I'm telling you. Say sorry or I may have to punish you."

At last, a voice in the crowd said, "Sorry."

A ragged chorus followed, though Devon saw that some stayed silent. Oh well. It was good enough for now. "There. Doesn't that feel better? Now, I think we should all have a big party with lots to eat and drink. I'll have a burger, please, and a big soda, and some ice cream."

"I'd like a burger too."

Everyone ignored Brandon, except for Devon, who firmly told him, "First of all, you can bring everyone back so that all my new friends can meet all my old friends."

Brandon stopped grinning after that. He became tight-lipped and sulky because he'd been pushed aside again. Devon almost felt sorry for him because that would've been the nice thing to do. Then again, he was Brandon. He wanted Auntie for himself, but he couldn't have her. All he could do was what she told him to do.

Tyler was tight-lipped as well. Unlike Brandon, though, he wasn't always trying to tell everyone else what to do. Because of that, Devon was much nicer to him. "Put a chair and table in the back of Brandon's truck, please. I want to sit there and watch everyone having fun."

By the time Devon was all set up in the back of the truck, with Auntie standing quietly by the open tailgate, her food and drink had arrived. The Boise crowd stood off to her left, and her newly returned flock stood off to her right. But no one was having any fun at all. The ogre might be gone and Brandon told off, but there still might be a fight. This wasn't good at all. What was needed was something to break the ice, like a court jester or something. As if by command, a man stepped out of the Boise crowd and stood exactly halfway between the two groups.

He gave Devon an expansive bow. "Your Highness. May I introduce myself? My name is Will, and I would like to entertain you. What would you like, I wonder—a song, a dance, perhaps a little magic?"

"Oh, magic please. I want to see some magic tricks."

"But of course. Your wish is my command."

The man approached the truck with an impish sidestep this way and a sidestep that way, and Devon fell in love with him instantly. Thin-faced with flaxen hair streaked with rainbow colors and freckled cheeks, his green eyes glinted with a promise of naughtiness and his smile with a promise to let her in on a big, big secret that only the two of them would know. From somewhere underneath his ankle-length black coat, he produced a big bunch of flowers, and then a stream of different colored kerchiefs, all of which he offered to Devon as if they were the most treasured things in all the world.

Wide-eyed, she left her chair to kneel in front of him and took them all, hugging them to her chest.

He then produced a pack of cards. "How about a

trick or two? Would your highness like to choose one?"

"Yes, please." With the flowers and everything else put aside, she watched him spread out the pack facedown before her.

Before she could choose one, though, a familiar voice butted in. "Hold on! Just who the hell are you?"

It was Brandon, of course. While everyone else watched from a distance—quite a few of them craning their necks as if they wanted to see some card tricks as well—he strode purposefully forward, all fired up for yet another confrontation. "Well? I said, who the hell are you?"

"I'm Will. I'm an entertainer. I like to make people happy. You look like you could do with some happiness right about now."

Will was right. Brandon needed an awful lot of happiness. Instead, he bristled with suspicion. "An entertainer! And you just happen to be here right now, do you?"

"Well, yeah. Why shouldn't I be? The people of Boise have a right to be entertained the same as everywhere else, don't they?"

"Well, yeah." Brandon almost mimicked him. "Everyone has a right to be entertained, I guess. I just happen to think if it looks too good to be true, it probably is, and you turning up right at this moment is seriously too good to be true."

Oh, dear. Brandon could pick a fight with his own reflection and never think twice about it. Why he wanted to pick a fight with Will when he was being so delightful was a mystery, not only to Devon but to Will as well.

Producing something wrapped in gold foil from his great big coat, he offered it to Brandon. "Be calm, brother. Chill. Have a chocolate bunny. Chocolate bunnies are everybody's friend."

Devon was instantly delighted. "Oh, please! Can I have one too?"

"But of course." Will offered her Brandon's since he didn't seem to want it. "Your highness has only to ask, and I will fly to the four corners of the Earth to seek it out for you."

As Devon took it and began to rip away the gold foil, Brandon could only stand, speechless and upstaged again. He wasn't the only one who looked decidedly unhappy either. With Ross recording everything at her side, Ali watched Will with her own pouty scowl. Behind her Tyler simply looked puzzled. Auntie was happy enough, though, so Devon was happy too. Also, she had her creamy, melting chocolate bunny to munch on, and she just knew that from now on Will was going to be one of her best friends.

Will must've known it too. Ignoring Brandon,

as everybody eventually did, he took control, facing the two still separated crowds. Half skipping and half dancing his way between them, he held out a hand to each of them. "Why all the long faces, people? Her highness wants everyone to be happy. You wouldn't want to disappoint her, would you? So let's all come together, then. Let's all be one big, happy family and have a party, just like Thanksgiving."

No one moved. They probably didn't like Thanksgiving. But Will wasn't going to be put off by that. Suddenly darting toward someone in Devon's flock, he grabbed a girl by the hand and dragged her over to the Boise crowd. "Come on. What have you got to lose? My name's Will. What's yours?"

The girl was unsure almost to the point of shyness. "Sage. My name's Sage."

"And yours is?"

The man they stood in front of looked as big and mean as the ogre. He was dressed much the same too, except for the bandanna tied around his head. But though he looked like an ogre, he chose to be nice. "Hey, how y'doin'? They call me Tank but my given name is Kirk."

"There." Will threw his arms wide for everyone to see. "That's how easy it is, people. All you gotta do is try. So come on, put on a happy face, and say hi to the person standing in front of you. You never know. You might end up spending the rest of your lives together."

With that, in dribs and drabs, people began to step forward, and slowly the two crowds came together. Devon smiled as she watched. Will was just the person she needed: someone who didn't constantly bicker with everyone else, someone who just wanted to make everyone happy like she did, someone God must have sent, just as he'd sent her Auntie. Now that she had him, he might be the only one she listened to, something the others must've thought of too because Ali now stood in front of her with a big frown on her face.

"Devon, sweetie. Didn't your parents ever tell you not to trust strangers?"

Ross, Brandon, and Tyler stood a ways back beyond her, with the last two frowning just as hard as Ali. Devon sighed a little because she knew they must've been arguing again. Grown-ups really ought to learn that sometimes things were exactly as simple as they appeared to be.

To Ali, she replied, "Yes."

"Good. Because we don't know who this Will person is. We don't know where he came from or why he's here or what he wants. You do understand, don't you, Devon? He might not be the nice, happy person you think he is."

"I understand. You think he might secretly be a

Nazi or work for the bad god CIA or something."

"Devon, quit it with all this Nazi stuff, will you—although the bad god CIA might not be so far out there. But no, I don't think he might secretly be a Nazi. I just think, well, you can't just go trusting everybody who walks up to you and makes you smile."

"Why not? I trusted you, didn't I, and you didn't even make me smile."

Ali bowed her head, muttering something Devon couldn't quite hear. It was probably something kids weren't supposed to hear, the kind of thing grown-ups said when they were trying very hard not to get mad. Devon waited because Ali would surely think of something to say that wasn't all just scolding.

"Devon. We all know God gave Auntie to you so you can make the world a nicer place. We're all here to help you. None of us would ever dream of trying to take Auntie away from you, but there are—"

"Brandon does."

"Brandon's an idiot!"

"So you don't like him either."

Ali struggled again. "I'm sorry. I shouldn't have said that—not to you, anyway. Besides, it's not about liking him or not. The man doesn't have a clue. He thinks he can just read it in a book and then go out and build it. Hasn't he ever tried putting a piece of flat-pack furniture together? And, my god, he's so smug with it too, like he knows it all, except of course he doesn't. He doesn't know who these people are. He doesn't know how they live or what they want. Maybe it's because he's never had to work for anything his entire life. Hell, he probably doesn't even know how much the apartment he lives in cost. It's just there because his trust fund paid for it. Now he thinks he can hand free apartments out to everybody because, y'know, they're just there. Nobody built them. Nobody services them. They just exist. Maybe … Oh, I don't know. The guy's just an idiot, and there you are, I've said it again."

"What about Tyler? Is he an idiot too?"

"Tyler? Tyler's a sweetie. He's a lot like you. He just wants to make everything better. But Brandon. Brandon wants to stand on the back of a truck and harangue a crowd, like Lenin. That's all he cares about."

"Who's Lenin?"

"Oh, he was some guy who caused far more problems than he solved, like they always do. But that's men for you. One day, sweetheart, you'll learn the same as the rest of us. If you want something really messed up, get a man to do it."

Devon nodded. That must be why God hadn't given Jesus an Auntie, because he was a man and God guessed he might mess it up.

CHAPTER TWELVE

After partying all afternoon, everyone decided to stay in Boise for the night. There was plenty of room, what with all the hotels being empty —and people in the Boise crowd knew exactly how to break in.

The next morning, Devon's flock became twice as large. Several more trucks and cars brought up the rear of the convoy, and a whole load of big, noisy hogs ran on ahead or flanked them. They were really just great, big motorcycles, so why they were called hogs was a mystery. Perhaps it was because they snorted so much. Some of their riders did too, but no one would tell Devon what that white powder was. All they said when she asked was, "Don't go there."

Heading southeast, they drove through flatlands of browned grass and scrub. Devon hardly noticed.

Will rode in the back of the bus with her now and he did a far better job of keeping her entertained than even Tyler had managed. The time flew by, just like the barely changing landscape, until midday brought them into Idaho Falls. Everywhere was empty, not a single living person to be seen, as if something had wiped out the entire population. But it was because of the evacuation, or so everyone in the bus thought as it pulled into a supercenter lot to park.

While most of her flock fanned out to find something to eat, Devon stayed where she was with Auntie sitting beside her. Tyler's friends would bring her something to eat and drink, so she was happy to sit and watch.

Will ran around buoying up the spirits of anyone who looked like they needed it, or perhaps he simply annoyed them. Ross casually recorded nothing in particular. Tank and Sage were getting along beautifully since their forced introduction. And Ali, Tyler, and Brandon stood in a knot on the far side of the lot. Even from this distance, Devon could see they were having a serious conversation—or probably just bickering again. She wished she could hear what they were saying, and then, all of a sudden, she could.

"So we're agreed then, right? He's an infiltrator."

That was Brandon talking, as forceful and argumentative as ever. Turning a wide-eyed gaze on

Auntie, whose big gleaming head was pointed in the group's direction, Devon was filled with wonder. "I didn't know you could do that."

Auntie, of course, said nothing, but Tyler said, "Well, yeah. I guess."

"You guess! Hey, if they're trying to infiltrate us, this isn't a game anymore. You do understand that, don't you? We gotta get serious. We gotta start making decisions and carrying them through. We can't be afraid to do what's necessary."

"And what is necessary? If he is an infiltrator, what exactly do you mean to do about it?"

Ali sounded coolly critical, remaining not in the least bit affected by Brandon's bullishness.

"You don't need to worry about that. Me and my guys will take care of him."

"Yeah. But that's the question I'm asking, isn't it? What exactly does 'taking care of him' mean? Are we talking about dumping him by the side of the road, or are we talking about dumping him in a ditch?"

On the other hand, Ali's words instantly affected Tyler. "Whoa, hold on a minute. We aren't about to start killing people, are we? What would that say about us?"

"It would say we're not playing games. If sacrifices have to be made for the greater good, then so be it. Besides, in case you've forgotten, Auntie's already made quite a few people disappear. What do you think? They all just went home to Momma or got beamed up to a UFO or something? We're already committed. We already got rap sheets. There's only one way we can go, and that's forward, like a shark."

Ali nodded, with just the smallest upturn of a smile. "Nice. You were gonna make the world a better place, and now you're a shark. You want my advice? You best not tell Devon that. She believes she's doing God's work."

"Oh come on. She might only be seven years old, but that doesn't mean she's all sweet and innocent. That guy in Boise was no accident. She told Auntie to do it. So long as she controls Auntie, this is about who controls her. If Will is an infiltrator, from the government or whoever, then someone else has figured that out too. So whadda you wanna do, huh? Wait around until we become surplus to requirements or act? I say we act. I say we let them know we're running things around here. I say we dump him, in a ditch if necessary."

"Hi."

This voice was new, and it wasn't inside Devon's head. As she turned away from her eavesdropping, all the other voices fell silent. Outside the back of the bus stood a woman, her hands thrust into the pockets of her jeans. Above them, she wore a checked shirt and below, a pair of low-heeled boots. Long brown hair reached down either side of her square face, and a bright and friendly smile wrinkled up her brown eyes.

"Hi. You're Devon, right? I thought I'd just come on over and introduce myself, what with you being all on your own and all. I hope you don't mind."

Well, she didn't look like a Nazi, and she didn't sound like a Nazi, in so far as Devon knew what Nazis looked and sounded like. Having just listened in on Brandon, Tyler, and Ali's conversation, though, it occurred to her that this woman might be something else. "I don't mind. Are you an infiltrator too?"

"Heavens, no, pumpkin. Where on earth would you get such an idea? My name is Annie Rae, and I'm just visitin' in Idaho. I was stayin' with a friend in Boise when they all just rolled on up and told us all to quit. Well, where I come from, we don't take kindly to the government tellin' us what to do, so me and my friend, we hid out until they left, and then we saw everyone havin' a good time at the bar, so we joined in. Then you came along and, my lord, you made such an impression on me. So tell me, Devon, that guy in Boise. Was that some kind of magic trick? Did you make him disappear, like behind a curtain or somethin', or did you really make him disappear, like forever?"

"I sent him to God. But that's okay. I'm sure God loves ogres too, unless they're really bad, of course. Are you bad?"

Annie Rae laughed. "My, such questions you do ask. Well, maybe. Maybe, just sometimes, I'm a little bit bad, but not so bad as the Lord wouldn't forgive me for it. We all got the right to be a little bit bad, don't we, so long as we're truly sorry afterward?"

"I guess."

Devon was beginning to like Annie Rae. She clearly wanted to be good with God as well, apart from the occasional little bit of naughtiness, which God was surely big enough to forgive. The same couldn't be said of Brandon, Tyler, and Ali. Still standing on the far side of the lot, they glared at the two of them like three evil witches trying to cast a curse or something.

Devon was about to find out what they could be so annoyed about, because they marched on over, as determined as an unwelcoming committee. They planted themselves firmly where they meant to stand, and Brandon started the unwelcoming. "Who the hell are you?"

"Oh, hi." Annie Rae told her story again with the same bright and open smile she'd given Devon.

"So where's your friend now?" Ali acted a bit like Brandon, talking to Annie Rae with the disdain she usually reserved for him.

"Oh, she ran off faster than green grass through a goose. When she saw that guy in Boise disappear, she turned as white as a sheet, and I haven't seen hide nor hair of her since. I think maybe she's back in her apartment hidin' behind the sofa with her cat."

"But you didn't. Why's that?" Brandon said, just plain cold.

"Well, as I told Devon, that thing made a wondrous impression upon me. Did you make it in a laboratory somewhere, or maybe in your garage? Because I've watched videos of what they can make robots do these days. It truly is scary to think what might happen if they turned bad on us, don't you think?"

Before anyone could answer, Will came bouncing over, full of puppyish enthusiasm and grinning hugely. "Hey, people. Is everybody happy?"

"No! Take a hike."

Poor Brandon. One day he might figure out no one wanted to play with the angry kid.

"Oh, dear. I think somebody's got their grumpy pants on. Hi, by the way. I'm Will. I'm an entertainer."

"Hi." Annie Rae introduced herself for the third time.

"Well, hi. Would you like to see a magic trick?"

"Yes! I'd like to see you disappear."

This second outburst from Brandon was enough for Tyler.

"Can we stop with this?" he said. "If we're all going to be here together, we can at least try to work together, can't we?"

Ali replied with a snort. "Yeah. Because that's been working out so well, hasn't it?"

Ross turned up, but that only gave Brandon somebody else to snap at. "Will you stop, for Chrissakes! Jesus, you don't have to film everything, y'know."

"Well, sorry." Ross stopped, but only for so long as it took to speak.

Devon sat quietly watching it all. She ought to be pleased, probably, because at least Brandon and Ali were now on the same side, almost. But then, of course, that was because they now had Will and Annie Rae to not like. Maybe they were infiltrators, which Devon guessed meant she ought to not like them as well, and maybe they weren't. She sighed because this was difficult. All these people squabbling and disliking each other wasn't going to make the world a nicer place. If they didn't stop, she might have to get mad with them. That would mean having to punish them, but, apart from threatening them with Auntie, she didn't know how to do that. She couldn't exactly send them to their rooms until they learned to be good.

One thing was for certain: no one was going to be dumped because Brandon said so. The only one who would be deciding things like that was her. Since they all seemed to need reminding of it, she looked down on them from her high chair and reminded them of something else too. "Why hasn't anyone brought me something to eat? Princesses can't be expected to think of everything, you know."

"Devon!" Ali sounded stern again, which was becoming increasingly annoying. "We've talked about this. You can't—"

"Oh, don't you never mind about that." At least Annie Rae was still smiling. "I think she looks real cute sittin' up there in that pretty blue dress and everythin'. So how about I go find you somethin' to eat, pumpkin? Would you like that?"

With a nod from Devon, she hurried away. Ali and Tyler glared and stared after her. Will pulled a flower from his sleeve and tried to find someone who was interested, and Brandon glowered at him because that was what he always ended up doing. This was going to be very difficult indeed.

An hour later, with everyone fed and mostly happy, the convoy set out again. North and east out of Idaho Falls and then east and southeast beside a river, they drove through fields and forest. Annie Rae had joined Devon in the back of the bus, much to the disgust of Brandon and, to a lesser extent, Ali. Tyler was more than happy to have her, though. With Will there too, along with Laura, James, and Madison, everyone was having a good time talking of this and that until Tyler suddenly turned serious. "So where are you from, Will? You never said."

"All over. Home is where I hang my hat, like in the song. That's how it is when you're an entertainer. You follow the crowd, just like lions follow the wildebeest. Rroarrr!"

He mock lunged at Devon with his hands curled up like claws.

She giggled because he was still the funniest one of them all.

Tyler had other things on his mind. "A lion, huh? Well, there are some people around here who think you're stalking us."

"Of course. I stalk my prey and kill them with laughter—a joke here, a trick there, and then I tickle them to death."

He reached out to tickle Devon and she giggled again.

None of the girls seemed to think it was funny, and even James watched coolly. They must be jealous because Will wasn't paying them any attention.

"Yeah," Tyler said. "I think they're more concerned

174

with why. We're not exactly meat on the hoof here, are we?"

At that, Will turned serious too. "Hey, the work is where the work is, man. I go where my agent sends me."

"That would be one way of putting it," said James.

To which Tyler added, "What he means is, some people think you might be here to spy on us."

"Spy!" Will laughed. "Let me guess. That'll be Brandon, right? Does he think I have a pen that fires poison darts, a watch that's also a camera, and my belt is really a ladder?"

"I dunno," said James. "Do you?"

"Oh come on, guys. I'm an entertainer. All I've got up my sleeve is a bunch of flowers. Besides, I'm not the only one who just joined up here. Why aren't you asking her if she's a spy?"

Will pointed toward Annie Rae, and all eyes turned to her. Devon felt sure she would deny it too because she was far too nice to be a spy.

Instead, she smiled disarmingly. "Well, I guess now's as good a time as any. I'm not here to spy on anyone, but I am representin' people who would very much like to help, people who have the resources to get you anythin' you need."

"What?" Tyler even went so far as to take his eyes off the road for a moment. "You're the infiltrator!"

"Oh, now, don't be so harsh. I think ambassador

would be so much more appropriate."

Here was another word Devon didn't understand. "What's an ambassador?"

"An ambassador? Why, pumpkin, an ambassador is a person who helps people be friends with each other, and the people I represent very much want to be friends with you."

"Okay. But why do they want to be friends with me? I don't know who they are, and before Auntie came along, I wasn't supposed to talk to strangers. So why should I be friends with them?"

"Because they've been watchin', and they're very impressed with the way you've brought all these people together in such a short time. They're also super-impressed with Auntie. She is such a wonder, a truly amazin' sight to behold. They would very much like to help you and her get to where you want to go."

"They do? Or do they just want to control me because that's how they get to control Auntie?"

Tyler glanced sharply at Devon, and she almost grinned at the sight of it. Yes. She had listened in on that conversation, but she wasn't about to tell him, or anybody else, how Auntie could do that. They'd just have to guess how she knew and then probably decide she was a lot smarter than they thought.

Meanwhile, James let out a snort. "Yeah, right. These people want to help her and Auntie get to where they want to go out of sheer goodness. Or do they want to help her and Auntie get to where *they* want them to go? And who are they, anyway, because you ain't exactly telling us, are you?"

"My, aren't you the suspicious one. That's okay. I get it. Truth is, I don't know who all of them are myself. I only get to meet the ones I get to meet, y'know. I can tell you they're not government, though. They're just concerned people, worried about where our country is goin' and thinkin' we could be headed for somewhere better."

"Well, phew. For a moment there I was beginning to think somebody might be setting us up to be their patsies."

"No, they just want to help, and now is the time, what with the government havin' its hands so full and all. But then, I suppose you don't know, do you, what with the little bubble they've been keepin' you all wrapped up in. You got half the country at a standstill. The cities are in lockdown. The National Guard is out in every state. The president has declared a state of emergency. There's even talk of martial law because so many people won't do as they're told."

James might still be full of doubt, but Laura seemed close to awestruck. "Really? My god, those hackers said it was crazy nuts out there, but people really are weirding out all over the place because of us."

"All over the place. That video you put out in Yakima got an awful lotta people fired up. Hard as the authorities try, they just can't stop people seein' it. Europe, Asia, Australia—it's everywhere. The global economy hasn't just caught a cold. It's bedridden. But that's exactly how you want it, right? Then you can step up with a promise of hope, equality, and a fair distribution of resources for all. That's why the people I represent want to help you, because you've achieved more in just a few days than they have in decades."

"Pleased to be of help, I'm sure. But it still sounds like they just want to walk in and take over. So how do we know they won't?"

Tyler didn't actually sound very pleased at all.

Devon wasn't too pleased either. Everyone just kept forgetting, so once more, she reminded them. "Because they can't. Auntie is mine. If they want her to be their friend, they're going to have to make me want to be their friend, and first of all, I want something better than this bus to ride in. I want something a princess ought to be seen riding in."

"And that, pumpkin, is exactly what I'll tell them. A princess ought to have a big, beautiful coach to ride in, and people to drive it and help her with all the gettin' in and out. Why, I'm sure they'll be just as happy as pigs in slop to oblige."

CHAPTER THIRTEEN

Rock Springs was just as empty as everywhere else. Since it was early evening, they stopped in the middle of the highway, with a hotel on one side and a supercenter one road over on the other. Almost everyone headed for the supercenter, and Devon used Auntie to make the locked doors disappear. She waited outside, knowing someone would bring her something to eat and drink. Pretty soon, they'd set themselves up in the parking lot with all sorts of garden furniture and everyone was enjoying the sunset.

Devon sat at her table with Ali, Annie Rae, and Tyler, feeling all warm inside at how wonderful it was. A few days ago, all these people might never have even met each other, and now here they were all partying together, and it was all because of her, just like Annie Rae had said. Well, God and Auntie had helped, of course, and if she could do this in just a few days, just imagine what she might do in the weeks and months to come. The entire world might become one big party with everyone getting along, just like God wanted.

Then, with the dusk closing in around them, someone decided to start a bonfire. Since a lot of people were starting to get noisy again, the mere suggestion was greeted with whoops and hollers. That must be due to all those bottles and cans they were emptying and then throwing onto a growing heap. Soon enough, all sorts of other things were being dragged out of the supercenter and piled up in the parking lot. Moments later it was ablaze, with flames climbing all the way up into the darkening sky. Fireworks followed, and Devon laughed and clapped as multicolored rockets exploded above her. After that came bangs of a different kind, and Ali, who'd been coolly but uncomplainingly watching it all until now, quickly became concerned. "Looks like they've found the guns. How long did it take Brandon to figure that one out, d'ya think?"

"Maybe it wasn't Brandon. Maybe it was some of our new friends from Boise."

Tyler was trying to sound convincing, but Ali didn't care. "Whatever. It's time we left. Come on,

Devon. Let's get you over to the hotel and all tucked up in bed for the night."

Devon didn't feel at all like going to bed, though. "Why? Everyone is having fun. I want to stay and watch some more."

"Sweetie," Ali said in her don't-argue-with-me voice. "It's all becoming a little rowdy, don't you think? What will Auntie do if she decides she doesn't like it? You don't want her to accidentally make some of your new friends disappear because she's scared, do you?"

Auntie was perfectly quiet, standing there behind them with the light from the bonfire reflecting off her great, silver body. She had gotten scared before, though, making people disappear when Devon hadn't wanted her to, like Melissa, for instance. Oh well. Maybe it was better to be safe than sorry. "Okay then. We'll go."

"Good. I don't know about you, pumpkin, but I'm feelin' a mite sleepy myself," Annie Rae said. "Let's go find ourselves some nice big beds we can have all to ourselves."

Annie Rae was a grown-up. If she was feeling so sleepy, surely she could go find a bed on her own. Devon didn't say any of that, though. She didn't want to be nasty when Annie Rae was being so nice. Besides, the thought of a big bed all to herself did sound rather nice.

With Auntie's hand in hers, she followed on as Ali, Tyler, and Annie Rae skirted their way around the merrymaking. It was all quite magical, almost like the elven fire she'd come across in the woods that first night. Still just a little disappointed, and even though no one was watching, she waved to them all as she left, quietly and wistfully wishing them goodnight.

They crossed a road, walked between some buildings, and found themselves back on the highway, where the vehicles in their convoy were parked nose to tail in front of them. As they walked beyond them, heading for the side road that would take them to the hotel, Devon saw someone lurking behind Brandon's truck, talking into a phone. No one else noticed. They were all too busy talking among themselves. Maybe this person was another spy. Maybe it was Brandon himself, although him being a spy didn't seem very likely, what with spies having to be all secret and not starting fights with everyone.

Wanting to know, Devon told Auntie to listen in. It wasn't Brandon. It was Will, the entertainer she now realized hadn't been entertaining anyone tonight. Whoever he was talking to, he didn't sound much like an entertainer either.

"I know … yes, yes, I know … Well, no, actually. I don't think you fully understand what's happening here. You've been emptying out towns and leaving all the stores full. These people are just taking whatever they want, whatever they need: food, drink, and now guns. You do understand, don't you? They're arming themselves … For god's sake, will you listen to what I'm saying to you? … Under control! What do you mean, under control? You're creating an army here, an army with more than a few ex-cons in it led by a seven-year-old girl who has a killer alien robot that'll do anything she tells it to. Which part of this doesn't have you reaching for clean underwear?"

He wasn't happy at all. That was understandable. Devon knew what not being listened to felt like. Not that she felt sorry for him, because now she knew for sure he was an infiltrator, a spy. Annie Rae was too, but she'd already admitted it. Now Devon began to wonder about Ali and Ross, because who knew what they might be getting up to in the back of their van with all that broadcasting equipment. That left Tyler and Brandon, but Brandon was an idiot, according to Ali, and Tyler was too nice. All the same, Devon was suddenly unsure as to whom she could trust outside of Auntie and God.

She would've liked to listen in on Will some more, but there wasn't time. Everybody else was walking on. That was probably for the best because she had an awful lot to think about. But it would have to wait for tomorrow, because now, they were entering the hotel and there were rooms to be chosen and Auntie to be squeezed into an elevator. On the second floor, Annie Rae took the room to the right, Ali the room to the left, Devon went with Auntie to the room in the middle, and Tyler took the room opposite. Everyone thought that would be safest, just in case anyone from the parking lot decided to bring the party with them. No one did, as far as Devon knew.

The next morning, it was easy to see why. Devon's entire flock was very quiet. They walked around as if they'd just been told the cat had died or something and drank an awful lot of orange juice which somehow made them feel better. Grown-ups could be really strange sometimes. Oh well. Devon sat at her table, quietly munching her way through a bowl of chocolate-flavored cereal, the milk turning all brown with it, as she looked out over the mess they'd made. Someone was going to have to clean it all up. It wouldn't be her, though. She was a princess, and princesses didn't do things like that.

An hour later the convoy set off again. With hog riders once more leading and flanking, they continued eastward with the highway snaking along beside some railroad tracks. The mood in the bus remained quiet. Almost everyone on board—Annie

Rae, James, Madison, and Laura—stared out at the endless grassland and hillsides to either side of them. Will seemed to have other things on his mind, leaving Devon unentertained and increasingly bored.

Tyler must've been bored too, because after a while, he started talking to himself. "I know we're supposed to be inside a bubble and all, but this is like the zombie apocalypse finally arrived."

No one answered, including Devon, although she did stop kicking her feet against the bottom of her chair.

"Maybe not," he continued. "Maybe it's because almost no one lives in Wyoming. I mean, look at it, a big country under a big sky, and not a living thing to be seen. Makes you sort of wonder what all those pioneers did for entertainment."

Devon twiddled her wand. She couldn't think of anything to say. Neither could anyone else.

The silence dragged again until Tyler carried on with his thinking out loud. "I've never understood zombies. They're dead, right? So how come they're still walking around? Their hearts aren't beating, so there's no blood supply, so how are they getting oxygen and all the rest of it to their muscles? And if they've been dead for six months or more, why haven't they all been eaten or just rotted away?"

Devon didn't know. She knew what zombies

were, of course. They were scary monsters that walked around eating everything they could catch. She didn't like them, especially when they could run fast. The good thing was it was all just make-believe, because God would never let that happen. Letting the whole world be overrun by things that just ate everything was silly. There would be nothing left to eat, and then they would all starve like those children in Africa. That didn't make any sense at all, especially since zombies were supposed to be dead people, and God surely wouldn't want all those dead people walking around.

Tyler must have been thinking something like that too. "Maybe it's all the preservatives they put in our food. Who knows how long a zombie could walk around for if it's been feeding on that all its life, and then they eat the living and get some more. Maybe that's what keeps them walking around as well."

So it wasn't God then. It was people putting pre ... preservatives ... into everyone's food. Devon hadn't heard of that before. Now that she had, other questions occurred to her, like why was her flock following her? They ought to be doing it because, like Auntie and her, they wanted to make the world a nicer place. Or maybe they were just zombies who'd eaten too many preservatives. If they were just zombies, all she had to do was keep feeding them, like pets, and they'd surely follow her anywhere.

That was interesting. That deserved to be thought about some more.

Tyler continued thinking out loud. "My god, look at it—grass, grass, and more grass. How could you even tell if a zombie apocalypse had happened? I mean, it's so dull even zombies probably wouldn't be caught dead here. I wonder how many words for grass they got in Wyoming? Like the Inuit and all those words they have for snow."

Tyler prattled on some more, but after a while, even Devon stopped listening. She just listened to the sound of his voice, which was somehow soothing, rather like the hum of the tires on the road. She tried to think about all those things she had to think about, but she couldn't. Her thoughts just kept slipping away from her, and sometime later, gentle shaking awakened her.

"Hey, sleepyhead. Did you have a nice nap?"

Stretching and yawning, Devon gave Annie Rae a big nod.

"Good. I think an awful lot of us needed that after last night's excitement. So here we are. We've just pulled up in Rawlins. How about we go stretch our legs for a few minutes before we head on out again? Would you like to do that, pumpkin?"

With another nod, Devon followed her out

of the bus, and Auntie squeezed through the door behind her. They'd parked outside a truck stop next to a gas station and convenience store to the south of the highway. There wasn't much else and, while some tried their luck at the convenience store door—Devon didn't take Auntie over to help them—the rest milled around or hung out together in little groups. That left the hog riders. Some of them gathered together with Brandon and a couple of his guys and engaged in what looked to Devon like the sharing of a secret.

Wanting to know what the secret was, she listened in, but only soon enough to hear the lead hog rider finish it all off. "Okay. We'll check it out north, south, and east. Anyone comes across anything, you head right on back and report it. We all good with that? Then let's get to it, people."

The hog riders roared away, leaving Brandon with that usual smug grin on his face. He was always happiest when he thought he was in charge. Certain of it now, he walked over to the convenience store, where someone had finally managed to force their way in, set two of his guys to stand at the entrance, and organized a line so that only a few people at a time could enter. Devon left him to it. Taking Auntie by the hand, she strolled among her people, saying hello and waving to them as she went, because that's what princesses did. Zombies or not, all of them smiled and waved back, and she was happy.

Minutes later, the hog riders from the south roared back, stopping close enough to Devon that she didn't have to listen in as Brandon rushed on over. "Sup guys? You find something?"

"Yeah, man. There's a goddamn state pen down there."

"With people inside?"

"Well, we didn't get too close, but yeah. I'm pretty sure there were guards on the rooftops, and maybe some other people as well."

"Other people? What other people?"

"Dunno. Could be National Guard, could be regular army—definitely some kinda military, though."

A crowd gathered around them, and Brandon paused to think. Ali and Ross arrived, with Ali thrusting her mic into the middle of them all. "Hey, guys. What's happening?"

"We got troops in a state pen to the south of us."

The hog rider's report made Ali pause too.

"Troops, huh? Well, maybe they're there to protect it. We know they're evacuating towns, right? Maybe they decided they couldn't evacuate the inmates. Maybe they brought troops in to keep the place in lockdown—not because of us at all."

189

No one seemed very convinced by that. Devon glanced around at them all; she'd never seen so many gloomy faces. Will should've stepped in and cheered everyone up, except he was nowhere to be seen. Before she could wonder why he wasn't, the rest of the hog riders came roaring back.

Their leader pushed his way through to the front of the crowd so he could report too. "We got troops in that town. The highway's blocked east and west. I mean, they got APCs and Humvees and all shit like that. Looks like we just rode into a goddamn ambush."

"So what do we do?" asked someone in the crowd. "We can't fight the army, even if we wanted to, and I sure as hell don't."

Murmurs of agreement came from all around, which at least woke Brandon up. Casting a gaze at all the dissenters with an expression that told Devon he was about to start another fight, he opened his mouth to speak, but Ali beat him to it.

"Well, they're right. We can't fight the army, even if we wanted to. Perhaps it's time to face reality. It was fun while it lasted, but now it's over. Let's not get ourselves in any deeper."

Brandon exploded. "Let's not get ourselves in any deeper! Oh, but you don't know, do you? They already tried to stop us once, halfway between Tacoma and

Yakima. You all remember that, don't you? How'd that work out for them? So this time they got APCs and Humvees. So what? We still got Auntie, and now we got guns too."

"Yeah," said someone else in the crowd. "We got shotguns and hunting rifles. They got assault weapons. How's that gonna work out for us, d'you think?"

Ali was up for another fight too. "Besides which, I do know. What do you think I've been doing since I joined your little revolution? I've been documenting it, just like you asked me to. I know all about what happened back there. I know all about how it happened too. It was an accident, children playing with fire. I've got the eyewitness accounts to prove it. They want this over too, y'know. I'm sure they'd be more than happy for everyone to just go home, what with the world out there falling apart around them because of us. Ask Annie Rae if you don't believe me."

Now that Ali had mentioned her, Devon realized she'd disappeared too. There wasn't time to think about that, though, because Brandon squared off with Ali again. "Really? You think they're just gonna let us walk away? I already told you, we all got rap sheets by now. You think they're gonna give us all free pardons? Dream on. We started this because we wanted to force them to build a fairer world. Well, if all you want now is a pardon, the game remains the same. You're gonna have to force them into it, and you can only do that from a position of strength. Walk away now, and you belong to them. Is that what you want? Well, is it?"

All those unhappy faces clouded with indecision. Zombies or not, they were waiting for someone to tell them what to do. Brandon and Ali had tried, but that hadn't really helped at all. That left Devon, but she didn't know what to do either.

Fortunately, right then the hog leader stepped forward. Having spent the last few minutes talking to his guys from the south, he planted himself firmly in the middle of the circle, making it very clear he wasn't going to be argued with. "This guy is right, y'know. You want something, you gotta be strong enough to take it. You gotta keep going or die trying. Hell, that's what this country was founded on, wasn't it? People saying to hell with that, and then dying to defend it? Well, I didn't join this little roadshow just to quit halfway through. Goddammit, I never quit on anything in my life. I never backed down from a fight neither. Besides, you all seem to be forgetting something. It ain't your decision. It's Princess Devon's because she's the one who's in charge here. She's the one we're all following, so why don't we ask her?"

Devon was amazed. Ali had once said much the

same but, from then on, she'd never really seemed to believe it. Here, at last, was someone who might, openly and honestly. She was Princess Devon. She was in charge, and now the hog leader was walking over and crouching down in front of her. He was very much like the ogre in Boise, except he had a ponytail, several rings through his ears, and a big mustache that drooped all the way down to his jawline, its ends twitching constantly as he talked. He wore leather too, a zip-fronted jacket decorated with chains over pants and boots. In spite of that, he was a lot less scary than the other one. He sounded a lot less scary too.

"So, sweetheart, whadda you think we should do? Should we keep on going or should we give up?"

Before Devon could even begin to think of an answer, it no longer mattered.

CHAPTER FOURTEEN

Canisters bounced across the lot, spewing forth a thick white smoke. Devon, along with pretty much everyone else, watched fascinated as the smoke spread out into an all-enveloping mist.

Then someone shouted, "Tear gas! Everyone get down and cover your faces."

How many people obeyed was impossible to tell. Devon stayed exactly as she was, holding Auntie's hand and wondering what tear gas was. To her, it was just a white mist that turned a very ordinary morning into something quite magical. The only person she could see clearly was the hog leader, and he was on his knees with tears streaming from his eyes, which must be why this white mist was called tear gas.

Then she forgot about it because Auntie suddenly became very unhappy. Her temperature plummeted.

The next thing Devon knew, coils of wire came shooting from every direction. They hit Auntie and huge sparks flew from their metal tips before they bounced off and fell to the ground. Quite why anyone would want to shoot coils of wire filled with electricity at Auntie, Devon couldn't imagine. Now that they had, Auntie was as cold as ice. Raising a hand, she shot bolts of red light in every direction. Devon could just about make out the figures she shot at. They were like ghosts in the mist, a phantom army of darkling knights that some evil prince or sorcerer had sent to kidnap both her and Auntie and carry them off to his brooding, misshapen castle sitting on a lonely mountaintop. Instead, one by one, they glowed and hissed and disappeared, and those that remained backed away.

Auntie scooped Devon up into her arm and followed, still shooting through the mist. When they emerged into clear daylight, Devon saw that all the men wore camouflage like Melissa's men had been. Unlike Melissa's men, they also wore masks which must be why none of them were crying—especially since they were making more mist and backing away into it. They must have thought it would make them invisible. It didn't.

Auntie kept shooting and more of them disappeared until Devon decided it was enough.

"Auntie, stop."

Auntie did, but whether it was because she'd been told to or because a vehicle appeared away to their left, Devon didn't know. It was a big vehicle with no windows and all sort of angular, like a boat someone had decided to add six big, fat wheels to. On top of it a robot man sat behind a big gun. As the vehicle slowed to a halt, Devon listened in, because the robot man was arguing with someone. "It's got the kid in its arms, sir. You want what, sir? You want me to shoot the kid?"

Devon couldn't hear the reply, but it didn't matter anyway. Auntie shot a blue ball at it, and the vehicle and the robot man all crumpled up, squealing and grinding into an ever-smaller ball until they disappeared, just like the agent's vehicle in Baker City.

After that, Auntie rapidly began to warm again. Since that must mean all the darkling knights and robot men had run away, Devon gave her a grateful hug. "Thank you, Auntie. Now let's go back to the others. They're probably wondering where we are, if they've all stopped crying, of course."

Back at the truck stop, everyone was busy wiping their eyes. That was because of the tear gas, or maybe because so many of them were now really, really unhappy. If it wasn't for the hog riders, who corralled them like a flock of sheep, they might've all run away, which wouldn't be good at all. Devon already knew that being nice wasn't always enough. Sometimes people had to be made to do what was good for them. Having the hog riders help her do that was better than relying only on Auntie. Unlike her, they couldn't just suddenly make people disappear.

What was not so good was that, with everyone gathered together, Brandon had decided to give another one of his speeches. Standing on the back of his truck with a clenched fist bobbing up and down, he was busy playing Lenin again. "Come on, comrades. This was the battle of Rawlins, and those who come after us will remember it just like they remember Lexington and Concord. They'll say we stood up against tyranny and we won. They'll say we stood together, that we weren't afraid and, because of that, they couldn't beat us. They'll say we chose to risk hanging together so we could hang them instead. They'll say …"

Devon stopped listening. An awful lot of other people weren't listening either. Brandon hardly noticed. He was too fired up with being the center of his own attention to notice the distant stares and darting glances. Devon knew what they meant. People were feeling guilty, afraid they'd done something so bad they were going to be called to see the principal and find their parents waiting for them. They needed reassurance, not another one of Brandon's—what was it Ali had called it?—oh yes, a harangue. No. What they needed was to hear the words of a leader who loved them, the leader God had sent to take them to a nicer world.

At her wish, Auntie carried Devon over to where she would be in front of Brandon, silencing him instantly. From there she looked out over her flock— her poor, frightened, little sheep. They gazed back, all waiting for their princess to speak.

"Don't be sad. We did a good thing today. They tried to hurt us, and Auntie punished them for it. Bad people, like bullies and Nazis, ought to be punished when they try to hurt people. They might not like it, but it's for their own good or they might go out and do something worse. God wants us all to be good and kind and nice to each other, but he punishes the bad people too, doesn't he? So long as we're all good, then, God won't mind at all if we help him punish the bad people, because how else can we make the world like he wanted it to be before people started being bad? I think we should all say thank you to God for sending us Auntie, and then thank you to Auntie for saving us, and then everybody cheer up and be happy."

"Hell, yeah." The hog leader stepped forward to throw in his ten cents. "I think everybody should take a knee and thank the Lord for our deliverance.

He has given us a mission, people, and with Auntie's help and Princess Devon to guide us, we shall not fail him."

Surrounded by his wolves, Devon's flock did as they were told. Some knelt immediately. Others hesitated, but slowly joined the kneelers. Brandon's guys were the last to go down, uncertainly holding out for something that didn't come, like Brandon picking another fight, perhaps. He remained silent, and Devon was pleased with that. The hog riders would do very well at keeping everyone in order without any of Auntie's little accidents. If they kept Brandon quiet too, well, that was just a big bowl of ice cream with chocolate sauce on top.

After about a minute of silence, with even the hog riders down on one knee, the hog leader rose to his feet, glancing around like he was a little lost himself. "Outstanding! So ... whadda we do now?"

He looked at Devon, and as the rest of her flock also rose to their feet, they looked to her too. Unfortunately, Devon still didn't know exactly what to do, but Brandon did, or so he thought.

"We need to keep going," he said. "We can't turn back now. The only way is forward, so we need to get moving. The more time we waste standing around, the more time we give them to prepare for another attack. This is a race. We gotta get ahead of them, outrun them and get to Washington before they can figure out another way to stop us."

Ali wasn't so sure. "That's all well and good, but don't you think they've already thought of that? Seriously. Do you honestly believe the president is still in Washington? Do you honestly think he's just sitting there waiting for us? And, wherever he is, do you honestly think the military doesn't already have troops deployed all the way between us and him? Come on, Brandon. Even with Auntie, we're outnumbered thousands to one, and we haven't even seen the air force yet. What if they decide to try and bomb Auntie next? What if they decide the only way to stop us is with a tactical nuke?"

"A tactical nuke! You think they'd use a tactical nuke against their own citizens?"

"Why not? Aren't you the one who keeps banging on about how evil they are, about how they're just oppressing us and turning us all into minimum-wage debt slaves? You push them hard enough, why wouldn't they resort to whatever it takes and then tell everyone how they saved the world and look at the price they had to pay to do it? Isn't that exactly the kind of lie you keep accusing them of?"

"How about a manifesto, then?" Everyone now looked at Tyler. "Well, why not? We've already put out Devon's appeal for calm, haven't we, but have we actually told them what we're about, why we're doing this? So why don't we tell them properly? Put out a manifesto, and then, when they can see we're the good guys, they'll rise up and join us. Then it won't matter how many troops the government has."

Ali's answer began with a dispirited sigh. "Because we can't. Unfortunately, our hacker friends aren't quite as good as they made out. They're still trying, but every time it looks like they might do it, they get shut down. My guess is every agency in the country is just sitting out there waiting for them and blocking them as soon as they show up. We're gonna have to find some other way of getting the message out."

"Well, great. So we've still got no communications." Brandon paused, looking momentarily lost. "What about Annie Rae then? If we're going to trust her, can't her people set us up with something?"

"If we're going to trust her." Ali cast a glance over all the watching faces. "Where is she, anyway? It's not like her to not be around after having gone to so much trouble to worm her way in. For that matter, where's Will? Why isn't he prancing around being annoyingly cheerful like he always is?"

Devon wanted to know that too. Quite likely they'd hidden when the attack began and they hadn't come back yet.

Brandon had another explanation. "They

probably both ran for it. They're both infiltrators, after all, so they probably knew what was coming. That sounds about right, don't cha think? Will was government anyway, so they must have warned him. As for Annie Rae, well, who wants to back a bunch of losers? Power is all they're interested in, so they'll probably sit back and wait for the next opportunity to come along."

"Oh wow. Aren't you just the cynical one? Everybody except you wants to seize power. Everybody except you wants to use Auntie to further their own agenda. It must be nice being so much purer than everybody else."

Brandon glowered, but before he and Ali could butt heads again, or Devon could lose her temper with it, the hog leader stepped in. "When you're done arguing! There's a simple truth here. We're all of us up to our necks in this, which is just about where they're likely to put the noose, and this little army of yours ain't gonna save any of you from it unless we put some backbone into it."

"Meaning?" Ali asked.

Brandon added, "Yeah. Meaning what, exactly?"

"Meaning you need to get some real fighters into this camp. We got weapons. We got Auntie. But no amount of firepower is going to win if we ain't got people willing to use it. We need fighters." The hog leader nodded southward. "Right over there is a state pen. There's gotta be a couple hundred guys inside who'd be more than happy to join us in return for their freedom."

"What!" Ali exploded. "You wanna release a couple hundred convicted felons—murderers, rapists, kiddy fiddlers, and who knows what else?"

But the hog leader wasn't listening. Instead, he turned to Devon. "It's up to you, princess. You want people you can rely on, they're over there. I say we go get 'em."

"No! Devon, don't listen to him. Those people he's talking about, they're seriously bad people who've done seriously bad things."

Devon didn't answer immediately. Ali might be right, but then, so might the hog leader. Or maybe, for once, it was Brandon. Being a princess was really hard when everybody kept saying different things, any of which might be true. But a princess had to decide, which meant figuring out who was more right than the others, starting with Ali.

"Who says?" she asked her. "Who says they're bad people? The people who put them there? But aren't those the bad people we want to punish?"

"No. Devon. Look. God, how do I explain this? There are bad people and then there are very bad people, okay? Besides, not everyone who put the very bad people in there is a bad person. Quite a lot of them are actually good people."

"Okay. But if it's the bad people deciding who all the very bad people are, doesn't that mean all the good people are working for the bad people, like Melissa was? If the good people know they're working for bad people, they can't really be good at all, can they?"

Ali hesitated, her face a picture of confusion.

At the same time, Brandon sniggered. "Oh dear. How you gonna get outta that one, sweetie?"

They were about to start bickering again. Devon wasn't interested. She had a new best friend now, the hog leader, and it was to him she turned. "I think we should go get 'em and give my army some backbone."

While Ali turned away, throwing her hands up in disgust, and Brandon sniggered some more, the hog leader took charge. "Well, all right, then. Come on, people. Let's roll."

He hurried away to call his riders together. Devon would've liked to listen in but Ali stepped in front of her again. "Devon, please, you cannot do this. It's wrong. Those people in there, they—"

"—will do what they're told. It doesn't matter what the bad people say they did because Auntie will make them be good. From now on, everyone will be good and do what they're told and stop telling me what to do. I'm the one God chose. I'm the one he gave Auntie to."

Ali gritted her teeth. Devon could see she wanted to say more but they both knew Devon wasn't going to listen. There was nothing more she could do but go to where Ross was stood recording it all and mutter her anger at him.

At the same time, Annie Rae reappeared, smiling innocently as if there was nothing at all for her to explain. Devon didn't quite see it that way. "Where have you been?"

"Well, pumpkin, I was keepin' out of your way, what with all those government troops tryin' to give you such a hard time. My people watched it all, and they were very impressed. In fact, they're prepared to offer you anythin' you want, within reason. All you gotta do is name it, and it'll be waitin' for you at the next big town we come to."

Brandon was quick to leap in. "Communications equipment. And gas masks, body armor, and some real weapons. Shotguns, hunting rifles, and good intentions are no match for what they're packing."

Annie Rae listened, then looked to Devon for confirmation. Whatever body armor was, she was happy not to argue. There was one thing Brandon hadn't mentioned though, so, just to make sure, she added the reminder, "And my new carriage, fit for a princess. You haven't forgotten about that, have you?"

Annie Rae smiled, sweetly reassuring. "Now don't you worry. Everythin' will be waitin' for us down the road. I just have to go put the order in, is all."

"Good. Have you seen Will? Because no one seems to know where he is."

"No, I haven't. I suppose he must be around here somewhere. I could go look for him if you'd like?"

"Don't bother. He probably left with his friends."

Even Devon knew what Brandon meant by that, but Annie Rae still put on a face that suggested she didn't.

"His friends? Well, I'm sure I have no idea what you could mean by that."

"You know very well what I mean. He was an infiltrator, someone they sent in to get close to Devon so they could try to influence her. Hell, they probably had an entire room full of experts and child psychologists and suchlike brainstorming the best way to do it, and what they came up with was a clown. You know that because you're an infiltrator too."

"Honey, I just came along to offer a helpin' hand. I've never been anythin' but upfront about that, and I've never once tried to tell Devon what to do. If you want to see that as some kind of infiltration, all I can say is perhaps somebody is just a little bit afraid of losin' their own influence."

Brandon instantly bristled. "I'm not afraid of—"

"Shut up!" Devon was so abrupt that it wasn't just Brandon who looked at her in surprise. "All you ever do is pick fights, and you're not even very good at it. I'm tired of it. If you don't stop, I'm going to get mad—really, really mad. Do you want me to get mad with you?"

Brandon didn't answer. He didn't have to. He was red-faced enough with impotent rage. Annie Rae simply smiled winsomely, and Tyler, well, he didn't seem to know what to make of it all.

CHAPTER
FIFTEEN

Most of the hog riders were ready, their hands filled with every shotgun and rifle they could find. A couple of them were staying behind with everyone else. That was because they had no weapons, or so the hog leader said when Devon brought Auntie to join him. She wasn't entirely sure of that. A lot of unhappy faces still stood behind her, so maybe the hog leader just thought they wouldn't be any good, which, of course, was why they were going to the state pen in the first place.

Three abreast they set off, with Devon in the middle, Auntie to one side, and the hog leader on the other. All the rest followed in a silent knot, the outlying buildings of the state pen slowly growing larger before them. The tension among them slowly grew, even beginning to affect Devon. It wasn't a nice feeling. Hoping to stop it before it could affect Auntie as well, she looked up at the hog leader. "What's your name?"

He looked down at her. "H. Everyone calls me H."

"Why?"

A deep-throated grumble was his first reply, like some grown-ups did when kids asked them questions they didn't want to answer. Then he looked down at her again. "It's short for Hillary. They said it means cheerful, but at the school I went to it meant getting the crap beaten out of you near every day, until I beat the crap out of one of them. From then on, everyone just called me H. But don't you go telling my guys any of that, okay? H it is, and H it stays."

Devon nodded. "Okay. H it is. So do you beat the crap out of lots of people?"

H laughed. "Only when I have to, princess. Only when I have to."

"Yes. I'm trying to teach Auntie to only make people disappear when we have to, but sometimes she gets carried away. It's difficult, isn't it?"

"Sometimes. But then, sometimes it's the only thing some people understand, so you just gotta do it even if you don't really want to."

Devon nodded again. H was clearly a lot smarter than Brandon. He might even be smart enough to help her teach Auntie. All Brandon could teach anyone was how to start fights. It could be he was that way because he'd been like one of those kids who'd beaten the crap out of H and no one had ever beaten the crap out of him. Perhaps if H was to beat the crap out of him, he might stop starting fights.

That was as far as Devon got, because now they approached the outlying buildings of the state pen. One stood on either side of the road, each with a parking lot out front. Each of those lots held a scattering of cars and trucks, and a number of men stood on the roofs, some of them dressed in black and some in camouflage. One of them had a bullhorn. While Devon and H's hog riders were still the length of the parking lots away, he roared at them, "That's close enough. This is a state correctional facility, and you are advised to turn around and leave. Do not make us use force against you."

Everyone stopped. Devon looked up at H.

"It's your call, princess. Whadda you want us to do?"

Devon took another look at the buildings and the parking lots and the men on the roofs. Then she looked up at H again. "Sometimes you just gotta, right?"

H nodded. "Sometimes, princess. Sometimes."

Raising her hand, Devon pointed at one of the buildings. "Auntie. Fire."

Soundlessly a green ball streaked out, and a great

chunk exploded out of the corner of the building. Debris showered and clattered all around, and little men flew through the air as well. That was enough for the men on the other rooftop. Picking themselves up and dusting themselves off, they hurried away as fast as the slowest of them could hobble before they too were sent flying. Auntie waited obediently to be told what to do, and Devon chose to let them go.

Behind her, the hog riders picked themselves up off the road, some of them saying, "Holy shit, man!" and, "Christ, did you see that?" and, "Dude, we're just gonna walk into this place."

In his own way, H seemed mildly impressed too. "Well, I guess we're cookin' with gas now."

Just to be sure, Devon looked up at him again. "Sometimes you just gotta, right?"

He smiled, just a little, then turned to the hog riders. "Okay. We'll give 'em a few minutes to pull themselves together and get clear, but everyone keep your eyes open, just in case. Then we go on. There's still an army waiting to be liberated."

Well, that was what H wanted to do, but not all the men left. Some lingered to help those from the destroyed building. H didn't like that at all. Devon could see it in the firm set of his jaw and the growing intensity of his smoldering stare.

At last she asked, "Should I tell Auntie to do it

again, just to scare them off some more?"

H shook his head. "Nah. We'll go round the other side. By the time we get back, we'll have an army, so they better be gone. Come on, people. Let's move."

Staying well clear of the men from the rooftops, who stayed well clear of them too, H led them onward. Beyond the buildings, they passed by a security point and walked between the gray blocks of the prison buildings. Everywhere was eerily quiet, so much so that eventually one of the hog riders couldn't contain himself any longer. "You sure about this, man? I mean, this place looks like a ghost town to me."

Looking up at the roofs, with Devon following his gaze, H absently replied, "Yeah. Maybe they did move all the inmates after all."

"How can that be? If they moved all the inmates, why were they defending the place?"

"Dunno. Maybe they got something else here they don't want anyone to know about, like that Area 51. If you wanted to hide something where no one would go looking for it, where better than inside a prison? That doesn't explain why there's no one on the rooftops, though."

"So what do we do?" asked another hog rider. "Go on or go back?"

"We go on. You'll never know what's around the next corner if you don't turn it. Could be a pot of gold, could be an ambush. So quit yakkin' and start lookin'."

As all eyes turned to watch the windows and rooftops, Devon once more felt their growing unease. To her, these tall, gray walls were like the sides of a deep, dark valley. At the end of it, there might be that great, black, misshapen hulk of a castle where all the black knights who'd attacked them earlier came from. Broodingly evil, it might even be perched on a lonely mountaintop, except there weren't any mountaintops so far as she could see. Whatever waited for them within, sorcerer or witch, its wickedness couldn't harm them because God was watching over them. Also, Auntie had warmed up almost to the point of disinterest again, and if Auntie saw no cause for concern, then neither would Devon, in spite of how the rest of them felt.

Minutes later, they emerged from the south end of the valley, not to any castle, just more flatness. Devon was almost disappointed until she saw what waited for them across an area of empty ground. Security fences surrounded a compound, within which sat more gray buildings. Squat and silent, no people stood on the rooftops or anywhere else that she could see. It was almost as good as a castle, and somewhere within it, possibly in some horribly dark and smelly dungeon, were all those poor little prisoners just waiting to be rescued.

H chuckled quietly to himself as he looked upon them too. "Well, whaddaya know? They went and built themselves a new facility. Must've simply abandoned the old one. Well, people, there's our army. Let's go get it."

Behind him, the hog riders all cheered up, their unease disappearing like a closet monster when the lights switched on. Devon smiled. They were her brave band of knights, every one of them ready to confront whatever lurked within, and she was their just-as-brave princess, fearlessly leading them across the flatness, with the help of H and Auntie, of course.

As they approached the fence, Devon didn't need to be asked, and Auntie obeyed. A blue ball caused an entire section of it to fold up on itself and disappear into nothingness. A second blue ball did the same to the inner fence. Through the gaps they went, heading straight for the nearest building. They didn't even bother looking for a way in. Auntie simply fired a green ball at the wall in front of them and blasted an opening into it.

Holding up his hand, H brought them all to a halt. The hole gaped in front of them, black as a pit with nothing moving inside. Something troubled him, which wasn't like him at all. Devon wasn't in the least bit scared. Auntie was here, and so were all her knights. Nothing inside that hole could hurt her, no matter how evil it might be.

H saw it differently, though. He crouched down in front of her. "Y'know, princess, I think it might be best if you didn't come inside with us."

He was worried for her, which almost made Devon want to give him a big hug. "But don't you need Auntie to open doors for you or make walls disappear?"

"Oh, I'm sure we'll figure it out. And if we do need any help, I can always send someone out to get you. So why don't you stay here, and don't talk to any strangers, okay?"

Devon gave him a big nod. "Okay."

H rose and led his riders inside. Devon waited with Auntie, hearing voices from within, along with occasional clatters and bangs. Slowly the sounds grew more distant until she was all alone in silence. She looked up at the big, gray walls. They would be an awful lot friendlier if somebody painted a mural on them with lots of flowers and happy faces. She looked around at the brown, dry and dusty flatness to either side of her. Somebody really ought to put some of those sprinklers in, and then make a lawn with some flower beds. Mommy would certainly have liked that—if Auntie hadn't sent her to God. She turned to look at the buildings behind her, the ones whose dark valley they'd walked through. They didn't seem quite so threatening now, just big, gray blocks beneath a blue sky, like boxes all stacked up with who-knew-what surprises inside.

She looked down at the dirt at her feet and began to trace patterns in it with her toe. Becoming engrossed, she knelt down and started to draw pictures with her finger. First of all, she drew big Auntie, with little her standing hand-in-hand beside her. Then she drew Tyler with a big, happy smile and Ali frowning, always frowning. Then she added Brandon with an angry face surrounded by little lightning rods for hair. Deciding she didn't like that, Devon scrubbed Brandon out and drew a tree instead. At least trees didn't go around arguing with everyone all the time.

Tiring of that drawing, Devon scrubbed it out and drew another one. Then she drew another and another until, after she didn't how much time, one of the hog riders returned.

He gave her a big smile as he stepped out of the hole in the wall. "You might want to step back a little, princess. We got close to two hundred guys comin' out to join us."

"Two hundred! Is that how many they had locked up in the dungeon?"

The hog rider shook his head. "No, they got an awful lot more than that in there. The two hundred are the ones who want to join up with us. The rest just wanna stay locked up in their little boxes and be told what to do for the rest of their lives."

Two hundred was good, a proper army fit for a princess, but an awful lot more would be even better.

"What if I went and talked to them? Because they're probably just scared, and I could tell them it's all right because Auntie will take care of us."

"Nah. H wouldn't like that. Besides, some of them might be scared, but others, they're mean, too mean even for us. They won't take orders from anyone, especially a little girl like you, even if you are a princess and all. Best to leave them be. Once we're gone, the guards'll probably come back and then their little world will be right back to where it's supposed to be."

That mystified Devon somewhat. "They won't take orders from anyone, but they'll wait for the guards to come back and imprison them again?"

"Yeah. The slammer'll do that to you, given enough time."

Since he seemed to know what he was talking about, Devon didn't reply. Besides, she could hear sounds coming from the other side of the hole in the wall. Ushered to one side by the hog rider, she and Auntie watched as first H and then a long line of men dressed in orange began to emerge. They were all so very colorful and different that Devon decided she might keep orange as their uniform. Then everyone would know they belonged to her. She would have to talk to H about it first, because another thing she decided was that she would put him in charge of them. Tyler was too nice, and it definitely wasn't going to be Brandon.

In the meantime, every man in orange who walked through the hole caught sight of Auntie and gawked at her wide-eyed, as they should. It wasn't every day someone got to see what a gift from God looked like.

After all the orange men had come out, H's guys followed. Some of them had new guns and big shields and helmets with visors that made them look even more like knights. It was just a pity there were no big horses for them to ride too, but then big horses were slow, and they already had their hogs. They'd be her hog knights and this would be her army—the hog knights and orange men all led by H.

As if he already knew, H immediately took charge. "Okay. Now we got you all out, first thing is you say hi to the person you owe it to. This is Princess Devon. Come on now, say hi."

Devon gave them all a little wave. "Hi."

There was a halfhearted chorus of replies. An awful lot of the orange men didn't seem at all impressed with the idea of owing their freedom to a little girl. Some of them might even be having second thoughts. Just in case they were, H was quick to follow up with, "And this is Auntie. Auntie looks after Devon. She's her best friend, so you all better be nice to her because, believe me, you don't wanna make Auntie mad. She's the one who made that hole in the wall."

All the orange men looked first at Auntie, and then at the hole in the wall. Whatever they might be thinking, they kept it to themselves, but it didn't matter. So long as they all understood what Auntie could do when she was being helpful, they might think twice about making her mad. As for everything else, well, Devon was happy to let H explain it to them.

"Okay. So first of all we go back to where the rest of Princess Devon's people are waiting for us. Then we head into Rawlins and get you some new duds. Can't have you all walking around looking like a bunch of escaped cons, can we, even if that's what you are without us. You all might like to remember that in the days to come. Okay then. Let's move out, people."

No one objected; no one complained. The orange men all moved off as they were directed, looking an awful lot like a herd of steers being driven by H's cowboys. A little concerned, Devon glanced up at him. She liked her orange men in orange, and she wanted them to stay that way. Oh well. She'd already decided to make H the leader of her army. If he thought finding them new clothes was the best thing to do, she wouldn't argue with him. It was only a little thing, after all, even if this was her army.

Fifteen minutes later, and with all the men from the rooftops having gone away, they were back at the truck stop. All those unhappy faces they'd left behind looked even more downcast when they saw nearly two hundred freed inmates walking toward them. Devon saw this and decided they all needed cheering up. That would've been Will's job except he was still nowhere to be seen. Perhaps he had run away. If so, she'd just have to do it herself. She climbed up into the back of Brandon's truck and then paused a moment to think about what she was going to say, all the while looking out upon her flock. To her left, her orange men stood tightly together in a mob. To her right stood the knot of her other followers, with Brandon in front barely even trying not to glower. Between them was another chasm, like the one in Boise, except Ali, Ross, and Tyler stood in the middle of this one, all three of them staring at her with eyes as emotionless as the lens of Ross's camera.

Auntie and H stood in front of her, Auntie quietly neutral, as disinterested as she could be. But

H, as if he already knew what Devon was thinking, loudly proclaimed, "Well, here we are, people. We just got a whole lot bigger, so why all the sad faces? We got ourselves an army, and they're gonna think twice before pulling another stunt like that. We're on the path to righteousness, and the road to freedom, so come on—smile, be happy, and come together like we got a purpose."

Greeted with silence, he might just as well have been drowning kittens. Once more it fell to Devon, but that was okay. She was a princess, and princesses were supposed to know how to make their people happy.

"I think, well, I think we should all cheer up, just like H said. I mean, God wants us to make the world a nicer place, and we can't do that if we're all walking around being grumpy, can we? So we should all have some fun; that's what we should do. We should all have another party, like last night, with fireworks and everything, and then we can all get to know each other and become one big happy band like Robin Hood and his merry men. They didn't let the big, bad sheriff make them unhappy, did they? No. They lived in the forest and had parties every night, and all the sheriff could do was get madder and madder because he was a bad person, and bad people don't like it when other people are having fun, so we should have fun because it will make the bad people really, really mad. That's what I think we should do, and then we can have some ice cream too, because I haven't had any today and I want some. Oh, and also, I want H to be in charge of all of you. He's going to be my first knight, and all the rest of you should do what he tells you to do. Also, now that there are so many of you, I think I should stop being a princess and be a queen instead. From now on, I want you all to call me Queen Devon, and we'll have fireworks and ice cream every day."

"HUA!" cried H, just to round things off. His hog riders replied loudly to a man. The orange men sort of raggedly joined in, but everyone else remained silent. For them, he might now have been strangling puppies.

CHAPTER
SIXTEEN

"What's the matter, pumpkin? You look so sad."

Annie Rae reached out and placed a hand on one of Devon's where it rested on her lap.

It was after lunch, and they were outside a bar with Ali, Ross, and Tyler. The troops had disappeared. Unless there were people hiding out, Rawlins was deserted, another ghost town. Free to do as they pleased, almost everyone else had gone shopping, which meant breaking into stores and ransacking them no matter what they contained. The occasional sound of smashing windows and people whooping as they burst inside wasn't what was bothering Devon, though. It was her orange men, who were the most enthusiastic shoppers. She might have put H in charge, but it was still her army, and she knew how she wanted it to be.

"Oh, I don't know. I liked my orange men being orange, that's all. Now they're all going to be the same as everyone else."

"Well, sometimes you gotta let people do what they want, y'know, even if it is like Black Friday without the credit cards round here. Otherwise, they might start to thinkin' you don't really care about them."

That didn't help very much. While she continued being a sourpuss, Ali wasn't helping very much either. "Really? Now you're gonna justify looting to her?"

Annie Rae ignored her. "That's okay, pumpkin. You can still call them your orange men if you want to. It'll be like the cavalry still being called the cavalry even though they don't ride horses anymore."

"They don't ride horses anymore." Devon was surprised, so much so that she forgot her sadness. "So what do they ride, then?"

"Why, pumpkin, they ride helicopters. They fly in where they're needed, and then they fly out again."

"They do!" That sounded really exciting—much better than riding around in the back of some old school bus. "Could we get some helicopters? Then we could fly in and fly out again too."

"Well, I suppose I could ask, but then we'd need an awful lot of helicopters for everyone to fly in. Besides, I've already ordered your new transport, somethin' fit for a queen. You wouldn't want to give that up for some noisy old helicopter, would you?"

There was that, even though Devon hadn't really meant for everyone to fly around, just her. Now that Annie Rae had pointed it out, she realized there would quite likely be another problem too. "I suppose so. Auntie doesn't really like helicopters or drones. She gets really mad when one of them comes by. I think maybe she's scared of flying or something. I don't know why. She must have flown down here from Heaven, or maybe she just fell. There was a very big splash when she arrived."

"Was there? Well that would make someone afraid to fly, I guess, but then I can't imagine Auntie being afraid of anythin'. She is very … comfortable in her skin."

"Comfortable in her skin." Devon frowned. "What does that mean?"

"It means she's happy being who she is. That's why she's content to stand there so big and silver and silent, except when someone annoys her, of course, and we can't exactly blame her for that, now, can we?" Gazing up at Auntie, Annie Rae frowned a little herself. "Yep, she's big and silver and silent, like anythin' could be goin' on in there. You ever wonder what she looks like on the inside?"

"No. God made her perfect, just like he made everybody else, because that way everybody could be happy like he wants them to be. When everybody else is happy, Auntie's happy too. I know that because I know when she's happy and I know when she's mad too."

"But how? How do you know when she's happy and when she's mad? Does she talk to you, like a voice inside your head or somethin'?"

"I just know, that's all, like I know when I'm hungry or thirsty or bored, which I am now, so can we go, please?"

With Devon becoming irritable, Annie Rae was quick to smooth her down. "Well, now, there's no need to get mad. I was just askin', that's all. You know what? I think somebody needs a nap. I think we oughta find somewhere nice and quiet, and then we can all sit out in the sun far away from all this excitement."

Devon didn't want a nap. As they all climbed onto the bus, she wanted to know why Annie Rae was asking her almost exactly the same questions Brandon had. He'd wanted Auntie for himself. Now it seemed Annie Rae was trying to do the same, except she was being a lot smarter about it. Or she was just trying to be nice. It was becoming increasingly hard for Devon to tell anymore. If Annie Rae did want

Auntie for herself, it would certainly explain why she wouldn't give her any helicopters. Just imagine how silly she would look if Devon was to fly away with Auntie—so long as she didn't just blow the helicopter up, of course—and all Annie Rae could do was stand there on the ground crying out for them to come back. Except, of course, none of that would happen because Annie Rae wouldn't give her any helicopters to begin with. Grown-ups could be really annoying sometimes.

For a short time, they drove around town until they found a small park across from some railroad tracks with a long, low building called The Depot in front. In the center of the park was a round paved area with benches around its edge. To one side was another paved area with a fountain in the middle. A gazebo stood on the other side with a little slide and some small trees scattered around.

While Ali, Ross, and Tyler sat on the grass in front of the bus, Annie Rae and Devon sat on one of the benches. Auntie stood nearby like a big statue, all polished and shiny, as if she was someone famous the town wanted to remember. Neither hot nor cold, she showed no sign of even noticing as Annie Rae placed an arm around Devon, pulling her into a gentle embrace. The sun was hot, and the air still. In that quietness, whether she wanted to or not, Devon drifted in and out of wakefulness as the day drifted toward mid-afternoon. When at last she was done drowsing, she sat up to see that everyone was still where they'd been. With a big yawn, she rubbed the sleepiness from her eyes.

"Hey, pumpkin. You all rested up?"

Devon replied with a simple nod, and Annie Rae was content to answer with a smile and a rub of her hand on Devon's arm. In that silence, she looked across to where Ali, Ross, and Tyler sat deep in conversation. Purely out of curiosity, she decided to listen in, hearing Tyler first of all. "We're getting pushed out. You do know that, don't you?"

"Oh, I know." Ali might be gazing off into the distance, but she was still very much part of it all. "This whole little enterprise is being moved in on by some seriously bad people, and I don't mean all those cons they just busted out of that pen. I don't know exactly who Annie Rae is working for, but I'll take a guess there are some billionaires out there who just can't wait to get their sticky fingers on the entire damn world."

"So what do we do about it?"

Ali shrugged. "I don't know what you and Brandon and all the rest of them are going to do about it. You heard him as well as I did. You all got rap sheets by now. You're all in it till the end or you face the music."

"But not you. Don't you have rap sheets by now too?"

"Not us, brother. We're a news crew, remember? We're here with the full knowledge and permission of the TV station we work for. We're just documenting it all."

As confident as Ross might be, Ali's answer came with a bitter laugh.

"Yeah. We're just documenting the slow decline of good intentions into tyranny. How much did I not think that was where this was going when we hooked up with you outside Yakima."

"And that's how you think this is all going to end, is it? In tyranny?" Tyler asked.

Again, Ali shrugged. "Who knows, what with all those people out there trying to stop it or exploit it. What do you think they're looking for in all this? To protect us? To save us? To give us a nicer world, like Devon thinks she's doing? Or are they all out simply to control us, all of them? I don't know. Maybe I'm being too cynical. Maybe there is still hope, the hope that this can still be what I thought it was going to be, just another virtue-signaling ego trip. You'd make it as far as the next state maybe, attract a little media attention, say your piece about how unfair the world is, and then everybody would just get bored and pick up some takeout on the way home. Of course, I didn't know the truth about Auntie then."

Tyler smiled. "Yeah, Auntie's a real surprise like that. We knew all the way back in Tacoma, of course. That's why we started out on this. So what did you think she was when you first saw her?"

"A publicity stunt," Ross said. "Someone, maybe even Devon's real Auntie, dressed up in a Halloween costume, the whole thing put together by Brandon and his band of useful idiots. Then she starts making SUVs and people disappear." With a slow shake of his head, he continued, "Man, I could hardly believe my eyes when I saw that. How in the hell does a seven-year-old girl end up with something like that, anyway?"

"Because God gave it to her," Ali said. "Or so she believes. Or it escaped from Area 51, if you believe Brandon. At least Devon doesn't know any better, but Brandon; too much money and too much time on his hands. He probably fills his days watching bullshit videos on social media and believing every word of it because he doesn't have the brains to realize all those videos are being made by people who just want the clicks, the ad revenue, or they're just as dumb as he is. I guess the Devil still makes work for idle hands, and social media was his gift from God."

Tyler goggled a little at that. "Wow. You really are getting cynical, aren't you? So if she isn't from God or Area 51, where did she come from? You still think she's alien?"

Ross shrugged. "What else is there? Yeah, I know. Now I sound like I've been watching too many bullshit videos, but seriously, what else is there? Either she's from this planet or she's not, and I'm pretty sure that level of technology ain't from around here."

Tyler wasn't so sure. "So where are they, then? I mean, you gotta think they'd have noticed one of their robots was missing by now."

"Maybe they have. Maybe they're sitting up there right now laughing their cotton socks off. Look, guys, we just gave a bunch of monkeys a gun. Should we take it away from them? Nah. This beats abducting them any day of the week."

"It doesn't matter where she came from," Ali said. "Brandon was right about one thing, at least. What matters is who controls her, and that's Devon. The only way this is going to end without something terrible happening is if we can convince Devon to end it. That's the only way ..."

Devon stopped listening, even more disappointed than she'd been before. Here she was trying to make the world a nicer place, and almost everyone she'd trusted to help her wanted only to control her, all except H. He alone had never once tried to tell her what to do, not so far, anyway. She had to do something about it. She had to make them understand absolutely and forever that the only person who was going to control Auntie was Queen Devon, and no one was going to control her.

"I want to go back. Now, please."

Annie Rae smiled down at her. "But it's so quiet and peaceful here. Wouldn't you like to—"

"I said now!"

Devon glowered, daring Annie Rae to say no, and Annie Rae understood, or at least she understood the slow turn of Auntie's great, silver head and her faceless stare. Devon felt her chill, Auntie's answer to her own unhappiness. It was only the very mildest for now, but Annie Rae didn't know that. She did know what happened to people when Auntie got mad, though.

"Okay, pumpkin. If you want to go back, we'll go back."

Collecting the others as they went, they climbed back into the bus and returned to the place where they'd eaten lunch. The scene that greeted them as they arrived was like a five-year-old's birthday party without any grown-ups. About forty people, orange men and a smaller number of Devon's original flock, had been drinking, and they'd left empty bottles strewn among broken glass, upturned tables, and other debris. In the middle of the street, two of the orange men wrestled each other, landing punches in stomachs and ribs.

Devon, already unhappy at how everyone thought they could just use her, was even more annoyed at this. She'd left them alone for not even an entire afternoon and now here they were like it was a schoolyard fight or something. If it wasn't bad enough that the two orange men were pummeling each other in the guts, most of the rest, including students from her original flock, stood around urging them on.

"Really? I don't think we want to be here."

Tyler almost whispered it.

Ali replied in kind. "No, we don't. Come on. Let's get back—"

"Yes, we do!" Devon was having none of it. This was pure disobedience, a level of naughtiness that went way beyond simply being told to be nice. Someone was going to be very, very sorry. With Auntie in hand and almost dragged along behind her, she marched up to the outside of the circle.

"Stop it! Stop it now!"

The circle opened up in front of her. A lot of faces that had been smiling and whooping a second ago glanced uncertainly at each other as they tried to avoid looking at her. Quite right too. They were bad children who knew they'd done wrong, and it was no use them looking all sorry about it.

Devon took a step forward, leaving Auntie to

stand behind her. "Didn't I tell you? Didn't I tell you to be nice to each other? Didn't I tell you we had to become one big happy band like Robin Hood and his merry men? God wants us to make the world a nicer place, and here you are all fighting and behaving like little babies. I wanted us to have fun. I wanted us to have a party with fireworks and everything, but now? Well, now someone is going to have to be punished, that's what. Someone is going to have to answer to Auntie so that everyone else remembers."

One of the orange men saw it rather differently. "Now hold on a damn minute. First of all, we were just lettin' off some steam, that's all. I been stuck in that pen for two years being told when to eat and when to sleep and when to shit. If I want to have some fun, if I want to get drunk and start a fight, goddammit I will, so secondly, who the hell are you to tell me otherwise?"

"I'm your queen and you will do what you're told."

The second orange man saw it differently too. "Yeah right. Some little kid is our queen, and we're gonna do what we're told. Whaddaya say to that, brother?"

"I say, hell no! I ain't takin' orders from no kid. Shit man, I'd almost rather be back inside than put up with this bullcrap."

The second orange man laughed. "I heard that,

brother. Seems to me like it's that stuck-up little bitch that needs some punishin'."

An awful lot of the other orange men laughed with him. None of Devon's flock did. They stood hesitantly, hardly daring to even look because they knew what the orange men didn't. Devon was too mad to even care anymore. They'd disobeyed her, they'd used bad language in front of her, and they'd laughed at her. Imperiously unforgiving, because sometimes queens had to be, she glowered at each of them in turn. "One of you will be punished. I don't mind which one. You choose."

In the deathly hush that followed, the two orange men looked at each other, still grinning. They didn't believe her. They likely never would. That only made Devon all the more sure that she was right. People who didn't believe didn't deserve to be treated the same way as people who did. In fact, not believing was probably where all the bad people came from, and no one could make a nicer world if they let bad people be bad.

Everyone else waited—the students morose and apprehensive, the other orange men in almost gleeful anticipation of exactly what this little girl thought she could do to punish them.

Before Devon could do anything, Ali rushed forward. "Now wait. Everyone just wait a damn minute. Devon, you can't do this."

"Why not? God gave Auntie to me. God wants me to make everyone be good, and if they won't, they should be punished. Don't you want people who won't be good to be punished, to answer to God for what they've done?"

"This has got nothing to do with God, Devon. This is what the Nazis used to do. Do you want people to start calling you a Nazi? If you do this, that's what they'll do. They'll start calling you a Nazi, and it won't matter how much you want to make the world a nicer place. All they'll see is you and Auntie making people disappear because they wouldn't do what you told them to do. Devon, please. You cannot do this."

But Devon could because she was sick of being told what she could and couldn't do. She was sick of being treated like a baby because she was only seven years old. She was sick of everyone trying to take Auntie away from her. Auntie was her gift from God, and if God thought she was good enough, then everyone else should too.

"Please, Devon. Don't do this."

Most of all, right now, she was sick of Ali's preachiness, like somehow God had chosen her. He hadn't and, without hesitation, Devon pointed a finger at her. "Auntie. Fire."

An instant later, Ali was gone, and the silence

that followed was like the world had turned to ice. No one moved. No one spoke. Devon turned back to look at the two orange men; neither of them was grinning anymore.

"I told you. One of you will be punished. Now choose."

CHAPTER
SEVENTEEN

"By my reckoning, we've lost over half. They just up and vanished during the night. I guess they'd rather take their chances with the authorities than ..."

H didn't need to finish. Everyone knew.

Immediately after yesterday afternoon's events, Annie Rae and Tyler had ushered Devon and Auntie away, taking them to a hotel for the night. They'd been subdued, barely speaking, as if they were tiptoeing around something unpleasant. Devon couldn't imagine what. Nothing had happened that hadn't happened before, in Boise and other places before that. They'd been happy enough with it then. Being unhappy with it now just seemed silly. Grown-ups could be like that when they were trying to pretend something wasn't what it was, and right now, that included Tyler.

"Word must've spread during the evening," he said. "Anyone remember if Ross was recording it? If that gets uploaded, we gonna have some serious explaining to do. Where is he, anyway? We're going to need him to help put this right."

"Gone," said H. "His van too, and all of those hacker guys as well. We need to get in front of this. We need some way to communicate."

Annie Rae was the only one who wasn't being silly. "Already taken care of. There'll be communications equipment waitin' for us in Laramie along with everythin' else." In answer to some curious looks, she added, "Hey, the people I work for are all good scouts. Be prepared, which for them means always have a backup plan in place and ready to go. All we need to do is put this behind us and get to Laramie."

"Good." Devon was beginning to feel a little left out, what with all these grown-ups talking over her again. "Let's get to Laramie, then, like Annie Rae said. I want to see all the new stuff she has waiting for us, don't you?"

They must've done, because no one argued with her. H hurried away to organize some extra transport and get everyone on board. Annie Rae took Devon to a big store for new clothes. She was bored with the ones she had—the ones Ali had helped her choose.

While they were inside, Tyler sat in the bus all on his own. His friends James, Madison, and Laura must've all run away too.

An hour later they were heading eastwards again through a familiar landscape of scrub grass and hills, sometimes distant, sometimes close-by. Brandon's truck no longer took the lead. No one knew if he was further back in the convoy or whether he'd run off too. Instead, H and two of his hog riders led them, with the rest spread out front and rear, just in case anyone was ahead or behind them. Once again they were alone, the highway and all the rest areas they passed by empty. No one talked inside the bus, but Devon was happy enough with that. If everyone wanted to walk around with long faces because of what happened to Ali, well, let them. Ali was with God now. If Devon had made a mistake, he'd surely put it right. It really was about time they all understood that.

When they came to Laramie an hour and a half later, Annie Rae directed them off the highway to a parking lot outside the Wyoming Territorial Prison. Another small convoy made up of a big RV, a van with a dish on top, and two panel vans waited for them. By the time they pulled in to park up beside them, Devon had her nose pressed against the window. She just knew that big RV had to be for her, and she was eager to see inside.

Eight men, all dressed like the unicorn killers in olive and camouflage with boonie hats and heavy boots, were lined up in front of it. Firm-jawed and flinty-eyed, every one of them looked determined and ready for business, whatever that business might be. Devon hoped it wouldn't be unicorn killing because she wouldn't like that at all, and nor would Auntie.

As Annie Rae led the way out of the bus, one of them stepped forward. He wasn't the tallest of them, but he was the broadest, with a hand almost the size of a plate that he thrust out for her to shake. "Hey. You must be Annie Rae. You can call me Bill."

"Hey. It's really great to see you. I had my doubts as to whether you'd make it or not, what with all the interference they're runnin' out there."

"Well, they tried. They got a whole ring of troops stopping everyone from getting anywhere near you. We had to try a few times ourselves. A couple of times we got stopped, even at night. We just told them we were a news crew. The dish on the van helped. Throw in some smart-talking and they just turned us around and sent us back. We got lucky the third time. We found a way through, crept past them with our lights off, and here we are to tell the tale."

"Well, there you go. I guess I shouldn't have doubted you. So did you bring everythin' I asked for?"

"All in the vans. We got assault rifles, RPGs,

grenades, even a couple of light machine guns. Plus we got the communications set up and the RV for the princess."

"Queen." Since no one else was correcting him, Devon insisted, "I'm a queen now."

Bill smiled down at her like a kindly old uncle "Well, I do apologize. And might I be permitted to shake Your Majesty by the hand?"

"You might." Devon reached out to have her hand swallowed up in his. "I'd like to see inside now, please."

"It would be my pleasure."

Bill stepped aside, sweeping out an inviting hand, and Devon felt very queenly indeed. She was probably going to like Bill a lot. He was a bit bearish, big and growly, but at the same time, rather cute and cuddly. If the rest of his men were like him, she would probably call them her bears. They would fit in nicely with her hog knights and what was left of her orange men.

She liked him all the more when she climbed up into the RV with him and Annie Rae following. Auntie stayed outside to keep an eye on everyone else, or whatever she used instead of an eye. Devon's own eyes grew wide when she saw the plush seating, the kitchen area, her very own little washroom, and the big double bed in the back with a TV so she wouldn't have to watch any more boring scenery.

"Well, pumpkin." Annie Rae stood in the doorway watching Devon jump on the bed just to find out how bouncy it was. "Do you like it?"

"I suppose." The bed wasn't that bouncy but it would do. Besides, there was something far more important to consider. "I don't think Auntie's going to be able to get in, though."

"I don't think she is. But then a proper queen wouldn't want just anybody in her private space, would she? Auntie can ride along behind in the bus and stand guard outside when we stop for the night, just like a bodyguard ought to."

"Well." Devon wasn't sure she liked the sound of that. She would much rather have Auntie close-by at all times. On the other hand, Annie Rae was right. A queen shouldn't allow just anybody into her private space. Besides, Auntie wouldn't be that far away, and Devon would always know whether she was happy or not. "Okay then. But if Tyler's still going to be driving the bus, who's going to drive me?"

"I will," Bill called from somewhere behind Annie Rae. "I drove it here anyway, and Annie Rae can keep you company while we're on the road. Now, how does that sound?"

It sounded good, so Devon nodded. She would have her own little family inside her own little space where no one else was allowed, exactly like a queen should.

With everything settled inside the RV, Devon followed Bill and Annie Rae back outside. There, Bill's men were unloading crates from the back of the panel vans and handing out guns to the orange men and hog riders. Some of the students took them too. Others didn't, including Tyler, who stood by the bus with a very long face, like someone had stolen his lunch money or something. Maybe it was Brandon, because there he was with his guys, all of them grinning as they brandished their new guns, like nobody's lunch money was safe anymore.

"Okay." A bit like H, Bill wasted no time in calling everyone together and taking charge. "Once we've handed out all the weapons, those of you who don't how to use them can line up for some basic training. We'll get around to organizing a chain of command later. For now—"

"A chain of command?" H strode purposefully forward with a new gun in his hands too. "Unless I'm missing something, we already got a chain of command here. Isn't that right, princess? I'm the first knight of Queen Devon's army."

"Hi." Bill smiled broadly, holding out a hand for H to shake. "My name's Bill, and I'll be taking charge of Queen Devon's security detail."

H stared at Bill. He stared at Bill's outstretched hand just sitting there between them. Then he looked to Devon, as expectantly as the silence that had settled around them. At first, Devon didn't quite know what to say. Bill appointing himself to be head of her security detail was as much of a surprise to her as it must be to everyone else. She had to say something, though, or the two grown-ups she now trusted the most might start bickering like Ali and Brandon. That wouldn't do at all.

"H. This is Bill. He's going to be looking after me from now on. You're still my first knight though, so I want you both to shake hands and be nice to each other."

Bill stood, without a trace of doubt about him. H pursed his lips, his fingers opening and closing on his brand new gun, the one Bill's men had just given him. He was probably thinking they might try to take it away from him, or he might be thinking Queen Devon had spoken so that was that. Either way, he met Bill's gaze again and, at last, reached out a hand. "Hi. So I guess we'll be working together from now on, then."

"Looks like it. Perhaps we should get to know each other. I got something to drink in the RV, if you're so inclined."

That was pretty much everything outside the RV

settled too. Once everyone had started to breathe again, most went off for some weapons training while the rest chose to sit out in the sun. Devon might have joined them, but Annie Rae had another idea. "How about we go for a walk, pumpkin? A young body needs exercise, especially after all that travelin' we been doin'. I know I could sure use some."

Well, that was okay. Devon didn't mind going for a walk. Auntie was coming too, of course—although she probably didn't actually need any exercise. She didn't seem to need much of anything. She just was— big and gleaming and always quietly watching and waiting, as if she always had been and always would be. She might be young. She might be old. She might not even have an age because angels were forever, and she was Devon's very own personal angel. Perhaps all angels were like Auntie, except for her having no wings, of course. Angels ought to have wings, but then, no one was supposed to be able to see them either, unless they wanted to be seen. There could be angels everywhere watching over everyone with no one knowing they were even there. As they walked side by side and hand-in-hand, Devon wished Auntie could speak. Then she could've asked why Auntie was letting everyone see her and what God was really like, and a whole lot of other things no one else seemed to know the answer to.

Annie Rae walked beside them to the sound of gunfire from the parking lot. Devon liked that. It was almost as if she was her new mom, and she was making sure nothing bad happened to her. Auntie was perfectly capable of doing that, but still, it made Devon feel happy. She hadn't really thought that much about her real parents since Tacoma. There was no reason to. They were safe and happy with God. Now she realized that in all the time she'd been busy saving the world there was something she'd been missing, something that Auntie couldn't provide. Annie Rae and Bill could. It was having someone close-by who wanted to protect her because they cared about her. Of course, God cared about her. He wouldn't have given her Auntie otherwise. It wasn't the same kind of caring as having a mommy and daddy, though, and Devon was suddenly glad they were there.

"Can we do something different later?"

"Something different? Well, I don't know pumpkin. What is it you'd like to do?"

"I don't know. How about swimming? Could we go swimming?"

"I don't see why not. We just have to find a place. That should be easy enough, and I wouldn't be surprised one little bit if a lot of the others would like to as well."

Devon wasn't so sure about that. She'd really just

wanted Auntie, Annie Rae, and Bill to go, but then she was a queen now, and she had to look after her subjects. "Okay then. Let's go after lunch."

"Well, consider it done, then. I'll talk to Bill when we get back, and I'm sure he'll get it all organized right away. Now, why don't we carry on walkin' round this piece of history? Maybe we'll find somethin' interesting along the way."

That didn't seem very likely. All Devon had seen so far was grass, trees, and wooden fences with a couple of large huts poking through. Annie Rae did her best, explaining how it was all supposed to be like an old frontier town, but Devon was too busy thinking about other things—like ice cream, and swimming, and how everyone was going to be happy because she said so.

By the time they had walked all the way around and back to the parking lot, the gunfire had stopped. Now everyone was sitting around in the sun, just chatting away as they waited for their queen to return. Choosing to give them all the good news herself, Devon climbed to the second step of her RV and called them all together. "I've decided something. Since everybody's been so good, I think we all deserve a special treat. So, after lunch, we're all going swimming."

Most of her followers cheered or applauded, and

she was pleased they liked their treat. Some didn't, though. They stood there with glum faces as if they'd just been told it was time to go visit the dentist, or something. Maybe they couldn't swim, or maybe they just didn't know how to have fun without getting drunk. They were mostly orange men, so it was probably the second, since they seemed to like drinking a lot. Never mind. They would learn because H and Bill would teach them. If they weren't enough, there was always Auntie. Devon had never seen her swim, so maybe she couldn't. She could certainly walk underwater though, just as she'd done when she walked out of the lake. That ought to be enough to convince anybody.

As the cheering subsided, someone shouted out, "We'll need swimsuits."

"And someplace to go," said someone else. "Unless somebody's been here before?"

With H standing beside him in a show of their togetherness, Bill partially raised reassuring hands. "It'll be taken care of. Lunch first. Then swimming. We'll meet back here in, say, two hours. By then H should've scouted something out. And remember, everyone—be vigilant. This town may look empty, but that doesn't mean it is. I wouldn't put it past them to try to pick us off one by one, so nobody goes anywhere on their own. Always go in pairs, or better yet, threes, and if you do come across anyone hiding out, bring them along too, but only if they want to. We're not gonna force anyone to join us. Is everybody good with that? Okay then. Back here in two hours, and all of you make sure to be careful out there."

Everyone hurried off, Devon's army in search of lunch and H and his hog riders in search of somewhere they could go swimming. Devon expected that she, Annie Rae, and Bill would do the same. Instead, while Bill's guys fanned out to stand guard around the parking lot, he and Annie Rae wandered off a short distance. They meant to have a private conversation, not knowing that Auntie could hear everything. Sitting down on the top step of the RV, Devon listened in too.

Annie Rae began with, "So what's it like out there?"

"Pretty quiet. A state of emergency's been declared. That's put a stop to nearly all the rioting and looting. Most people are sitting at home waiting to be told when it's safe to come out again."

"So the whole country's in lockdown, all because of us."

"Well, yes and no. The whole country's in lockdown, sorta because of us but not. This is all just a hoax, disinformation. Somebody went and got creative with CGI, and his name's probably Yuri. Don't cha just love that whole reds under the bed schtick? It's the gift that just keeps on giving. They got half the country distracted and confused, and the other half saying it's the End Times. Hell, they even got some people claiming Auntie is a Nazi robot sent down from Hitler's secret moon base. Of course, that might be us, because we're pumping out our own disinformation too. By the time we're finished, even the president won't know what to believe ..."

Not understanding any of that, Devon stopped listening. There was a whole afternoon of swimming to be thought about, and a swimsuit to be chosen, and soon, please.

CHAPTER EIGHTEEN

Laramie lay behind them. A few more had joined them there: stay-behinds and hide-outs who'd evaded the evacuation. But a few more had disappeared in the night, which Devon found disappointing since they'd all had so much fun in the afternoon. H had found them a swimming pool on the east side of town in among all the university buildings. Devon had swum and splashed with Annie Rae while Auntie stood guard over them. Sometimes she got splashed herself, but she simply shrugged it off, or she might have done if she'd cared to. Devon laughed at that and splashed her some more. After a while, she stopped bothering, since Auntie clearly wasn't going to join in no matter how much fun it might be.

Now the road hummed beneath the RV. Devon

sat up front next to Bill and Annie Rae sat behind. The highway stretched out before them through the same unending scenery, but Devon hardly noticed. She was enjoying how she could look down on the road ahead and at whatever was in front of them. H and two of his hog riders made a V formation like the head of a spear. That's what Bill said, anyway. Tyler drove the bus immediately behind them with only Auntie for company, and the rest of the convoy followed: buses, trucks, cars, and vans all filled with Devon's army.

The other thing Devon really enjoyed was being alone with Annie Rae and Bill. They were almost her new mom and dad. Only one thing was missing to make it all perfect.

"Are you married?"

"Are we married?" Annie Rae couldn't have been more surprised. "Why no, pumpkin. We only just met yesterday."

"Well, I know that. I meant are you married to someone else."

"Not me. Not anymore, anyway."

The satisfaction in Bill's words mystified Devon. He couldn't not want to be married. Everyone wanted to be married, because that was how mommies and daddies were made, and then they had kids and they all lived happily ever after. Devon wanted to know more, but she didn't quite know how to ask. Fortunately, Annie Rae wanted to know more too.

"Separated or divorced?"

"Divorced. She said, 'Let's get married and see the world.' She never said anything about the lawyers in between and how I'd be seeing the world to get away from them. Last I heard she married some other sucker, and now he's paying for her kids. Well, good luck to 'em. So long as their bloodsuckers can't find me, I don't mean to bear any grudges. So how about you? Married, divorced, or just not interested?"

"Near miss. Y'know, the high school sweetheart deal. Long story short, I got out just in time, and I've never been back. I got to see the world too. Not bad for a small-town girl from way down south, right?"

This conversation was becoming far too grown-up for Devon. Also, Annie Rae might not want to be married either. Well, that wouldn't do at all. It was time they both knew the perfect future she had planned for them all. "I think you should get married."

"What?" Bill cried.

Annie Rae added, "Whoa. Where did that come from?"

"Why not? You like each other, don't you?"

Beneath Devon's steady gaze, Annie Rae struggled for words.

"Well ... yes ... but ... it's not as simple as that. People don't get married just because they like each other. They have to be in love, like your mom and dad must have been."

"Not always. Princesses sometimes have to marry people they don't like unless a prince turns up to rescue them, which usually does happen, but not always. If a prince doesn't turn up, they sometimes have to run away and hide, like they do when the king marries an evil stepmom. But that's only when they have to marry someone they don't like, and you do like each other, so that's okay then, isn't it?"

"Well." Bill struggled for words too. "We may have to think about that one, princess. It's not something anyone should rush into, y'know. You wouldn't want to end up with an evil stepmom and an evil stepdad as well, would you?"

"No. But, then, you're not evil. Evil stepmoms are trying to steal the kingdom, and you're not trying to steal anything, are you? You're just trying to help me and Auntie do what God wants us to do. But okay then. I'll think about it too, because there are lots of things that will have to be done, like dresses and flowers and a band and invitations, and a big, big cake, and then we can all be the royal family, and everyone will be happy because everyone loves royal families."

Bill and Annie Rae exchanged a glance, the sort of glance grown-ups exchanged when they wanted to say no, but couldn't quite figure out how to say it nicely. Maybe they just didn't understand.

"I want us to be together, that's all, just the four of us."

"Oh, pumpkin. You're not afraid we're going to leave you, are you?"

"No. I just want us to be happy, the four of us together without everyone else always getting in the way."

"Well now, we can surely do that, just the four of us, anytime you want. All you gotta do is say the word. Bill will find ways to keep everybody else busy. Isn't that right, Bill?"

"You betcha. Lots of things need doing around here, and I'm just the man to do it. By the time I'm finished, Queen Devon will have an army she can be proud of."

That sounded wonderful, truly everything Devon could wish for. A queen should have an army that made everyone else see how important she was. More than that, though, she liked how Annie Rae and Bill were so willing to help. They weren't always finding fault like Ali had done, or arguing all the time like Brandon did. They really were almost like her new mom and dad, except for not being married, of course. That was something Devon would have to work on. For now, she accepted it with a big nod.

"Okay then."

"Well, okay then." Annie Rae and Bill exchanged another glance. This one looked an awful lot like they were relieved about something.

The rest of the journey passed largely in silence. Devon hardly noticed. After she'd worked on it, and Annie Rae and Bill had been made to see how wonderful it would all be, she wanted to be ready. A wedding would be pretty and magical, and it might be exactly the kind of celebration everyone needed right now. Since she was their queen, she could even marry them herself, although someone would have to show her how, since she'd never really paid that much attention at any of the weddings she'd been to. Then again, she could just be the maid of honor, because it was usually a pastor who did that sort of thing.

Confident it would all sort itself out, Devon set the whole thing aside when H brought the convoy to a halt. They were coming up on Cheyenne, and two of his hog riders waited for him in the middle of the highway. By the time Bill, Annie Rae, and Devon reached them, H had already heard what his two guys had to say. Devon could see from their grim faces that something serious must've happened. Since Bill was now her almost new dad and her head of security, she waited for him to take charge.

"What've we got?" he asked.

"We got a roadblock up ahead. Looks like the Magic City don't want us stopping by."

"How come? Shouldn't they have been evacuated like everywhere else?"

H shrugged. "Dunno. My guys didn't get too close, but they think they're probably some sort of militia, not military. Maybe they refused to leave. They're packing heavy enough for it, so far as my guys could tell."

Now as grim-faced as the rest of them, Bill didn't reply. Whatever a militia was, it must be pretty scary if he didn't know what to do. Besides, Devon was more concerned with something else. "Why is it a magic city? Is it full of castles and wizards and dragons and stuff like that?"

Annie Rae smiled down at her. "No, it's just a name they gave it a long time ago, like they call New York the Big Apple even though there isn't really a big apple there."

At the same time, H was voicing his own concerns. "So what do we do? Go on or go back? Going back is going to mean a pretty sizable detour."

Well, there might not be a big apple in New York, but that didn't mean there wasn't magic in Cheyenne. Since Devon knew grown-ups were perfectly capable of lying when it suited them, she decided there was only one way to know for sure. "We go on."

Everyone looked at her.

"We go on. That's what I've decided, so that's what we'll do. Auntie will come too, and so will everyone else, and then I'll talk to them. If they're nice, they'll listen and let us stop by. If they're not, well then, it's my army, and they'll let us stop by because I say so."

All the grown-ups exchanged glances, now more troubled than grim, but Devon had made her mind up, so that's what they'd do. Bill was the first to accept it. "Well, okay then. Let's go visit with all the nice folks in Cheyenne. There's nothing that could possibly go wrong with that, right?"

Everyone agreed, which was to say no one objected, though they could have been a little happier about it. All that the nice folks in Cheyenne needed was to have everything explained to them, and then they would be happy too.

The convoy moved on, within minutes coming in sight of a large interchange. A line of vehicles with an awful lot of men standing behind them was parked across both sides of the highway and to either side. To Devon, this didn't seem so bad. She'd tell them all to stop being so silly, that she and her army were only there to free them from all the bad people who made silly laws and any other Nazis that might be hanging around. Then they'd all be on their way to Washington to tell the president to stop being bad as well. If they wouldn't listen; well, then they must be Nazis too, and it was her duty to free the good folks of Cheyenne from them.

As Devon stepped down from the RV, she thought-called out to Auntie. In barely more than a moment, her great silver hugeness stood at Devon's side and, hand-in-hand, they walked toward the line. Behind them came Bill and Annie Rae, with H marshaling a steadily increasing number of Devon's army behind them. The men behind the vehicles watched, standing their ground with tightly grasped rifles and shotguns, despite the glances that showed some of them weren't sure about this at all.

About fifty feet from them, Bill placed a hand on Devon's shoulder. "Okay, princess. That's close enough."

At the same time, a man stepped out from behind the vehicles. An awful lot like Bill, he was stocky but taller, but with just as determined an eye and a rifle held firmly in his hands. "I don't know exactly what it is you folks think you're doing, but you're not wanted here. So move on, north or south, we don't care, but east into Cheyenne you ain't going."

Just as resolutely, Bill held his gaze. "Why's that? We aren't looking to cause you any trouble. All we want is somewhere to eat, and then we'll be out of your hair."

"You wanna eat? Find somewhere else. Now move on and do it fast. We don't want things to get ugly around here, but we will protect our town."

"No one wants things to get ugly, brother. Just a quick stopover and we're gone. No trouble, no threats, no problem."

"No trouble, huh? Like what happened to that reporter and that other guy afterward? Yeah, they showed us that when they told us to get out of town. Y'know what we said? We said no. This is our town and we ain't givin' it up to no kid with some ragtag army, no matter how scary that thing's supposed to be. Hell, they might even have made that whole disappearing thing up just to scare us into doing what we're told. Well, we can make people disappear too, or at least stop 'em from being a public nuisance. So why don't you take your freak show someplace else before anyone gets hurt?"

"Don't you want to be saved?"

Devon's question took the man by surprise, but at least he looked at her at last.

"Saved! Saved from what?"

"From the Nazis, of course."

"Nazis! You people are crazier than a box full of monkeys. Now get outta here. I ain't gonna tell you again."

With both his hands gripping that rifle really, really hard, he looked really, really mad. Or maybe he was just really, really scared. Cheyenne must be absolutely packed full of Nazis for him to be so scared. There couldn't be any other reason for it, so now it was up to Devon to reassure him, to tell him how she and Auntie were going to make all the Nazis go away, and then he could be happy again. She took a step forward, with Auntie beside her, meaning to show him how Auntie wouldn't hurt him. Before she could take a second step, two shots sounded from somewhere among the militia. Devon heard them sing and splat as they hit Auntie in the chest. There they sat, just as Melissa's had done, little metal pancakes that even as she watched were slowly pushed out by Auntie's resilient skin until they fell to the pavement.

Her reply was no surprise at all. Chilling into a deep freeze, she swept Devon up into one of her arms while the other began firing blue balls. Militia vehicles scrunched and screeched into nothingness, leaving the men behind them standing frozen in disbelief. At the same time, everybody else started shooting too, with people on both sides shouting and ducking while bullets whined everywhere. None of them came close to Devon, maybe because Auntie was protecting her, now with red balls that were making militiamen glow and hiss.

Just as quickly as it began, it was all over, with what was left of the militia hightailing it toward Cheyenne as fast they could go. Most of Devon's army cheered and whooped. Some didn't, among them the people Devon trusted the most: Bill, and H, with H the first to speak.

"Well, that was easy enough."

"Maybe." Bill's attention was fixed on what was left behind. Bodies lay all around, some militia, some Devon's army. Some were crying out for help. Others weren't moving at all. This wasn't like Auntie making people disappear. This was blood and pain, like falling over and cutting a knee. Devon felt sorry for them. She even felt a little guilty, even for the ones who'd fought against her, except, of course, it wasn't her fault. It wasn't Auntie's fault either, not this time. They should've listened and joined with her against the real bad people. Oh well. God would understand. He was probably sorting it all out right now.

"Maybe?" H cast an uncertain glance toward Cheyenne. "What? You think there's more of them just waiting for us to come on in, like this whole thing is some kinda set up?"

Bill shrugged. "Could be. They just showed us they're prepared to fight. If only one in ten of the citizens come out to defend their town, that's an awful lot of opposition without the military even being involved."

"So whadda we do? Go on or go around?"

It was most unlike H to sound so unsure, but that was okay. Sometimes a queen had to be sure for everyone. Besides, Devon still wanted to see why someone had called Cheyenne the magic city. "We go on. That's what I decided, so that's what we're going to do."

"Well." Now Bill was sounding unsure too. "Perhaps we ought to stop and think this over. There's no sense in going looking for a fight, not until we've—"

Well, this wasn't what Devon wanted: both of her most trusted people failing her like everyone else had done. Sometimes a queen just had to cross her arms and put her foot down. "They ran away, didn't they? That's because no one can stop Auntie. No one can stop me. We go on because I say so and because that's the way to Washington, and that's where the president is."

It was true. No one could stop her, but that didn't stop Annie Rae from trying. "Of course we're goin' on, pumpkin, but there are other ways to Washington. Bill is right. There's no sense in goin' looking for a fight when we don't have to. Discretion is the better part of valor, after all. So—"

"I don't know what that means. It sounds like something grown-ups say when they don't want to do something but won't just say so. Well, I've decided we're going that way, so that's the way we're going. I'll go by myself if I have to, and Auntie will come with me. If you're all really here to do what God wants, so will you."

Once again, Bill was the first to accept it. "Well, okay then. Before we all go rushing off though, there are matters to attend to here. Some of you guys start moving the bodies. Line them up by the side of the highway. Anybody got any medical or first aid training?"

Several hands went up, among them Tyler's.

"Outstanding. You all stay here and tend to the wounded. We'll leave half a dozen guys to look out for you, and the bus. Patch them up as best you can, then come on in after us."

A lot of those with their hands up looked relieved. Some of those who hadn't put their hands up looked like they wished they had. Devon wasn't concerned for them. It was leaving Tyler behind that suddenly bothered her. He'd been one of the first to follow her in Tacoma. He was also almost the only one who'd never criticized her or tried to tell her what to do, like he was the older brother she'd never had who just wanted to look out for her. A queen should have a prince by her side, someone who was kind and caring and never nasty to anyone. When she was old enough, maybe she ought to marry him, and then he could help her make sure that everybody was happy and had everything they wanted.

That was yet another thing to be thought about later, though. For now, the highway was being quickly cleared. As much as Devon wanted to get on into Cheyenne, Bill still wasn't ready. He was busy moving among the rest of her army, talking to various people, pointing this way and that, and nodding when they were in agreement. Devon could've listened in if she'd wanted to, but she decided not to. Whatever he was telling them, she was sure it would all be for the best. In fact, her royal family was shaping up rather nicely, what with Tyler at her side and Bill and Annie Rae standing behind her. Everyone would love them, and anyone who didn't must surely be a Nazi, but Auntie would see to them.

Satisfied at last that everything was ready, Bill briskly made his way back to report. "Okay. So we're heading on into Cheyenne, but at a walking pace. Most of our people will be flanking the vehicles with H's guys fanning out in front. If they got any surprises waiting for us down the road, I don't mean to just walk into them. I've told everyone to be on the lookout—eyes peeled and ears pricked. That way we should spot them before they can jump us."

"Okay. And Auntie and I will lead the way."

Bill and Annie Rae exchanged a glance. Whatever was on their minds, neither of them chose to say anything.

CHAPTER
NINETEEN

For more than an hour they walked, taking the highway north of the railroad tracks into the center of Cheyenne. Auntie carried Devon most of the way because she very quickly became bored of walking. H's hog riders spread out in front and to the side, reporting more roadblocks with occasional shots fired. The defenders of Cheyenne were keeping their distance for now, but still, Devon's army was watchful and edgy. Bill meant to keep them that way, urging everyone to keep their eyes open and their powder dry.

Devon didn't know what he meant by that, but she kept her eyes open too, increasingly disappointed at the ordinariness of it all. At first, the city was nothing more than a sparse succession of hotels interspersed with diners and auto sales outlets. Further in, the buildings crowded together and grew taller with all sorts of bars and small stores along the sidewalks. As far as Devon could see there was no magic here at all, until they came to a square with a big sign over its entrance that said it was the Cheyenne Depot Plaza. On either side of the entrance sat a giant cowboy boot, both of them painted up with pretty pictures. Devon looked around. Not only might there actually be a giant cowboy but also he might be quite annoyed that someone had painted all over his boots. That was silly, though. If there was a giant cowboy, someone would've noticed by now.

After setting watches at all the surrounding intersections, Bill, Annie Rae, and H came together with Devon and Auntie. Once again, H sounded concerned. "So far so good, I guess. We've reached the center of town, but they're all around us. So whadda we do now?"

Bill was more relaxed. "They might be all around us, but they're not coming at us. That meet and greet we just had must have significantly discouraged them. If they're going to keep their distance, we'll just pass on through, nice and quiet-like."

That was a little disappointing. Devon still wanted to talk to those people and make them see the good thing she was doing. Much worse, though, was that Bill seemed to have forgotten about Tyler.

At least Annie Rae hadn't. "What about the others? We're not just gonna leave them behind, are we?"

"No. We'll send someone back, tell 'em to haul ass on in here. So long as the citizenry don't decide to try for another Lexington, everyone else can take a break."

That cheered H up immediately. "Well, okay then. Anyone see any coffee shops on the way in? I don't know about you, but I could certainly use something to wash the trail dust out of my mouth."

As two of the hog riders roared back down the highway to call in Tyler and his group, others went looking for coffee. Devon sat on a wall by the entrance to the plaza, with Auntie standing close-by. She'd ordered ice cream and soda, and then waited and waited. Tyler would've brought it already, but there was no point in getting mad. He would be here soon, and she'd probably give him a hug just to let him know she hadn't forgotten about him. It was important to let people know they hadn't been forgotten about, otherwise they might get mad and walk out and never come back, and Devon didn't want Tyler to do that. In fact, what with the town being so peaceful and all, they probably should never have left him behind. Someone else could've looked after the wounded, after all.

Annie Rae returned, bringing ice cream, soda, and

coffee with her. "Here we go, pumpkin. Chocolate chip, just like you asked for."

"Thank you."

Devon began to eat, barely noticing the coldness of the ice cream or the bits of chocolate that were the last to melt. The quietness had all of her attention. Since Boise, every place they'd come to had been empty. Only in this town had there been anyone to meet them, and they fought against her. It didn't make any sense. She'd made that speech after Jake and his friends had arrived, the one everyone had thought was wonderful. She'd explained how God wanted everyone to be nice to each other and how he'd chosen her to make it that way. Yet still they ran away or fought against her. Maybe they hadn't seen that speech or they hadn't thought it was wonderful. If only they'd listened, she could have explained it to them again. Then a worse thought occurred. Everyone had a choice, like all the people who'd chosen to follow her. Maybe these people had chosen to do what the bad people told them to do, and that was very difficult to understand.

"Why don't they like us?"

"Why doesn't who like us, pumpkin?"

"The people in this town. Can't they see we just want to make the world a nicer place? Don't they want to live in a world where everyone is good to each other and has everything they need?"

"Well, people aren't all the same. For instance, I'm not you and you're not me. Because people aren't all the same, they all have their own idea of how the world should be."

"But why? I mean, when God made everything, he must have known how he wanted it all to work, mustn't he?"

"Yes, but God also gave us free will, so we could think for ourselves, and sometimes we get it all wrong. Sometimes we mess it all up."

"So God made a mistake, then."

"No, no, God doesn't make mistakes. God wanted us to think for ourselves. It's just that we're not always very good at it. Everyone wants to live in a nicer world, and everyone has their own idea about how to do that. Sometimes those ideas are good, sometimes they're not, and it's not always easy to tell the difference."

"And that's why God gave Auntie to me, because everyone should stop trying to have a better idea than him and just do what he says."

Annie Rae paused, her brow furrowing like she didn't quite know what to say. Then it didn't matter. The hog riders returned. Roaring up to Bill as if they meant to run him down, they leaped off their machines. As Devon listened in, one of them reported, "They're gone. We searched all around but there's no sign of them. The bus, the dead, the wounded, all the people we left with them, they all just up and disappeared like nothin' ever happened."

Disappeared! Devon leaped down from the wall. Taking Auntie by the hand, she hurried over to where Bill was standing as if now he didn't know quite what to say either.

She did. "Where's Tyler?"

The hog rider glanced nervously at Auntie. "Dunno. They're all just gone. All of them."

"Goddammit! I should've seen that coming. Someone took them. Any clue as to who? The militia, the military?"

The hog rider shrugged in reply.

Bill wasn't the only one getting mad.

"I want Tyler back. I want Tyler back now!"

"Goddammit!" With Bill giving way to exasperation, Devon went unheard.

"I said I want Tyler back! Now!"

Annie Rae reached out a calming hand. "We all do. But, pumpkin, we don't—"

"No! I want Tyler back now. Tell them to give him back."

Annie Rae's hand, already shaken off, hovered open-palmed in midair. She was not the only one shocked by Devon's outburst. Bill, H, the two hog riders, and just about everyone else within hearing distance stood frozen and staring as if she'd just shouted out a very bad word, like those people who lived on the street sometimes did. Devon didn't care. All she could see were people who weren't paying her the attention she deserved, people who weren't doing what she told them to do, people who would let bad people do bad things unless they were made to stop them.

Madder still because of it, she pointed randomly at a nearby building. "Auntie. Fire!"

A green ball flew and the building exploded, with everyone nearby ducking for cover as a shower of debris rained down on them. Driven on by the sight of it, she pointed at another building and then another, each one of them also exploding and showering debris all around.

As she pointed at a fourth, Annie Rae spun her round, demanding her attention. "Devon, stop. This isn't the way to get Tyler back."

Giving her all the attention she could possibly want, Devon glared. "Let go of me. I want Tyler back. Go tell them if I don't get what I want Auntie will blow everything up."

"All right. We'll send someone to talk to them, but you have to stop doing this."

"Why? All I want—all God wants—is for people

to stop being mean to each other, but no one ever listens until Auntie is mean to them. Well, I want Tyler back, and I'm going to let Auntie be mean to them until they give him back. Go tell them that."

Bill immediately motioned to the two hog riders. "Go! Go!"

"Go where?"

"Anywhere. Just find a roadblock and talk to them. Tell them what she just said and pray they're the ones who took Tyler because God alone knows what's about to happen if they aren't."

The two hog riders roared away down a side street.

For the next half hour or so, Devon stood, immovably furious. With her arms tightly folded and wearing a pout that dared anyone to talk to her, she waited. Bill, Annie Rae, and H moved away and were now deep in conversation. Devon could've listened in, but she didn't care what they were saying. She'd told them what she was going to do. If they didn't do what she told them to, she was absolutely going to do it. The same went for everyone else. She saw them, all creeping around like mice as they tried to avoid attracting her attention. Good. So they should, otherwise she might have to punish them all.

Well, not all of them, perhaps. That wasn't such a good idea. She didn't want to lose the rest of her army, like all the ones who had run away in Rawlins. She'd have to choose which ones to punish. They would have to be the most disobedient ones, like Brandon, if he was still here. He'd been disobedient right from the start, always arguing and picking fights and causing trouble. She could definitely punish him, and everyone else might even thank her for it. There had to be others too: trouble makers, big mouths, the snarky ones, and the ones who didn't really believe in her at all. She'd have to find them and then maybe punish them all together at the same time with all the proof of their badness laid out for everyone to see.

Since he'd appointed himself head of security, Bill would be the one to hunt them down. If he said no, maybe she would punish him too, but not now. Now the hog riders were roaring back, bringing someone with them, someone dressed in camouflage like all those people at the roadblock. He looked as nervous as many of them had been, glancing around at all the people staring at him as he climbed off the back of the hog, until he saw Auntie. Then he just stared at her, as if everyone had become invisible to him. Even Bill, H, and Annie Rae, until Bill clicked his fingers in front of the man's face. "Hey. You're talking to me, not that."

That earned Bill a glance, after which the man's eyes fell upon Devon. Half as tall as her again and with a round and thinly bearded face, he wasn't much more than a kid himself. Devon didn't care about that. "Where's Tyler?"

"Dunno. I ain't seen no one called Tyler."

"But you took him. We left him to look after all the hurt people, and you took him."

"Not us. We ain't been back there since we quit. Musta been the military. They're all around, just outta sight. You best talk to them if you can find them."

"But you're talking to them, right?" Bill said. "You must've been when they tried to move you out. You can talk to them for us, then, tell them we want our people back."

"Can't. We ain't seen them since we refused to leave. They said if we were dumb enough to stay, then we were on our own. Greatest fightin' force in the world, right, and they're afraid of a little girl and ... that."

"Yeah. Well." Bill cast a glance of his own at Auntie. "We still want our people back, so perhaps you find a way to talk to them. If you need any convincing, take a look at the three buildings that aren't here anymore. I can't guarantee there won't be more, or maybe worse."

"Why? Why you puttin' it all on us? We didn't take 'em. We don't know anythin' about it. And if you wanna talk to the military so bad, there's a TV station up the road a ways. Go make a broadcast. They'll see it. You could even make it like one of them appeals and include a contact number. That way they can call you up directly."

Throughout this exchange, Devon's stare had not wavered, with the man hardly daring to look at her. "I don't believe you. I think you're a liar and liars are bad people."

She raised her arm, all the way to its accusing finger, but before she could speak Annie Rae laid a hand upon it, gently forcing it down as she crouched before her. "Devon, don't."

This was what Ali would have done, and Devon turned her stare onto Annie Rae. "Why not? If bad people aren't punished for doing bad things, everyone will start doing bad things, won't they?"

Annie Rae looked a little lost. "Well, that's one way of lookin' at it, I guess."

"No. That's God's way of looking at it. People who do bad things get punished. They get to stand before God, and then God decides whether to let them into Heaven or not."

"Yes. Sort of. But didn't God give you Auntie so you could help him? God has lots of other things to take care of, lots of other people to look after. You don't know this man is bad. You don't know this man is lying to you, and you're not really helping God if you send all the wrong people to him, are you?"

"Well." Devon hesitated. Grown-ups always made things so much more difficult. "But God must've known that before he gave Auntie to me. He must've known that I'm only seven and that I would probably make mistakes."

"That doesn't mean you shouldn't try not to make mistakes, though, does it? You don't want God to come take Auntie away because you weren't tryin' hard enough, do you?"

"No." Devon looked down at her feet, beginning to feel as if she'd somehow done something bad. It couldn't be that bad, though, because God hadn't come to take Auntie away. Since that was true, maybe she hadn't done anything bad at all. It was just Annie Rae making her feel bad, or confusing her. Annie Rae was right about the rest of it, though. She didn't know this man was bad or that he was lying to her, not for certain anyway, and maybe she could try harder so God wouldn't have so much to do.

"Okay then. He can go. We'll go to the TV station and talk to the military instead."

With that decided, Bill wasted no time organizing everything. "Get him back to his people. Do it fast. Then get back here. Everyone else, we're moving on, so start getting busy."

A little later, the convoy walked its way on through Cheyenne. This time they left no one behind, with everyone, including the hog riders, ordered to stay close-by. The militia no longer posed a threat, or so Bill and H had agreed, but the military was still out there, and no one could know how close they were or how ready they were to pounce on stragglers.

After an hour of walking through suburbs and past an airport, during which Auntie ended up carrying Devon again, they came to the TV station. Inside, some of Bill's guys set about figuring out how to get everything up and running. Soon enough, they stood Devon in front of a camera with the studio behind it packed with all her followers who weren't guarding the perimeter outside. Annie Rae stood next to her, just in case she needed any help, although they'd already talked about what she might say. It'd all been written up for her on a teleprompter. While Devon was meant to read from it, she had her own ideas as well, things she hadn't told Annie Rae she might say. Once the countdown reached zero, they wouldn't be able to stop her, so, looking squarely into the camera, she took a deep breath and began.

"Hi. My name is Devon. I'm seven years old. I have a friend. His name is Tyler. Some bad people came and took him away. I don't know why they did that, because he's really nice. He's never hurt anyone, and now I'm really scared because I don't know where he is or what they're doing to him. Bad people shouldn't be allowed to do things like that. They should be stopped and punished and made to feel really, really sorry. I want to stop bad people from doing bad things, but I'm just a kid. I shouldn't even be here. I should be in school learning stuff, like the names of places and how things work. Instead, I'm here asking all of you why the bad people always end up running everything.

"Because no one stops them, that's why, and they ought to be ashamed for it. So I say shame on you. Shame on you for not stopping the bad people. Shame on you for not caring and making a little kid like me have to do it instead, me and Tyler and all my other friends. But it's not too late. You can still help us. You can still show that you care. If you've seen Tyler or know where he is, please call the number below and tell us. And if you're one of the bad people who took him, call us and tell us why. It's not too late to make everything good. Give Tyler back to me, and I promise I will forgive you."

With the video on continuous repeat, very soon the phone started ringing. Someone answered it, putting it on speaker so everyone could hear. Some of the people who called were nice, saying things like, "Oh, sweetheart, that's so sad. I really wish I could help," and, "I don't know who Tyler is but I really hope you find him. And you're right about the bad people. We should feel ashamed." Others were not so nice, saying things like, "Y'all just a bunch of nutjobs, that's what you are. Y'all just want to destroy our country," and, "Shame on you for using a little girl like that. She doesn't know what she's saying. It's all you people."

As for the military, or whoever the bad people were who took Tyler, Devon and her army waited, and waited, and waited.

CHAPTER TWENTY

They waited till the next morning, at some point growing tired of the calls, the good and the bad. Those who took Tyler hadn't replied. Devon was disappointed. No one had helped, in spite of all the nice things they'd said. As for all the people who'd said nasty things, now she knew there were an awful lot more bad people in the world than she'd thought. No wonder God had wanted someone to help him sort it all out, especially if he was as busy as Annie Rae said he was. From now on Devon would try much harder. She didn't want to waste his time by sending him good people by mistake, not now that she knew how many bad people there were out there.

After breakfast, they quit Cheyenne. With the bus gone, Auntie had to ride in the back of one of Bill's panel vans, but that was all right. She didn't mind. Bill drove the RV again, with Devon sitting next to him and Annie Rae behind. There wasn't much conversation because Devon didn't really want to talk. Watching the road ahead of them and the hog riders out in front, she answered anything said to her with nothing more than a yes or no, or sometimes she didn't answer at all. There were more important things to think about than Bill and Annie Rae's obvious concern, like how was she going to get Tyler back, and what kind of an example should she make of the bad people who took him? Letting Auntie simply make them disappear was hardly good enough. She wanted them to be really, really sorry right there in front of her, and then have to apologize to God as well.

Nearly five hours later, through more small towns and a Nebraska landscape that was hardly different to Wyoming, they came up on Kearney. The convoy stopped just before the interchange, a lake to either side of them, and Bill and Annie Rae got out of the RV to speak briefly with H.

When they returned, Bill gave Devon a confident smile. "We're going in nice and slow again, keeping everyone close-by. Doesn't look like there should be any trouble but who knows. We don't want another Cheyenne on our hands."

If he was talking about losing Tyler, Devon most

certainly didn't want another Cheyenne. If he was talking about some local militia lying in wait for them, well, as far as she was concerned, they were the bad people who made nasty phone calls. Auntie would deal with them quickly enough.

Through the interchange they went, with people walking on either side of the vehicles. Beyond it, hotels and restaurants lined the road. As soon as the convoy was neatly parked up in the lot of one of those restaurants, Bill called everyone together. "Okay. Go find lunch, but don't go too far, and don't wander off alone or even in groups of two or three. The more of you there are together, the less likely they are to try and take you. One hour, people. Then we move on."

Devon went with Annie Rae, Bill, and his guys to a nearby restaurant. Auntie stayed in the panel van, since she didn't eat anyway. A few others came with them, and they quickly forced the entrance and fired up the kitchen. While she waited for whatever they were going to serve her, Devon gazed out across the wide highway toward the building on the other side. It wasn't all that interesting, but then she wasn't really seeing it anyway. There were too many questions she still didn't have answers to, like how to get Tyler back, and how best to stop all the bad people from being bad without making God mad enough to take Auntie away.

Unable to find any answers herself, she looked to Annie Rae, who was sitting opposite. "If I don't send all the bad people to God, what should I do with them? I mean, I can't just tell them to stop. That's what the police do, and no one listens to them."

"Well. I guess it depends on how you tell them. If you give people a good enough reason not to be bad, most of them will be good."

"But that's called bribery, isn't it? Stop being bad and you can have a cookie. So what happens when you run out of cookies?"

Annie Rae glanced across the highway at the same building Devon hadn't really been seeing. She didn't appear to be seeing it either, what with her thinking so hard about an answer. "That, pumpkin, is why we have the police. If people refuse to stop bein' bad, the police come and arrest them and then they get sent to jail."

"So we need somewhere to send them, like summer camp but without all the fun stuff. Then we can teach them to stop being bad, and they're not allowed to leave until they promise, even when all the cookies are gone. That way we won't have to bother God, and he won't get mad at us."

Whatever Annie Rae might have answered, it was lost as a burst of gunfire broke the silence of Kearney. Every head in the restaurant snapped around, Bill's guys already reaching for their weapons. More gunfire followed, a *rat-tat-tat* that became continuous even as it became louder. By the time Bill had led his guys out into the parking lot, all the scattered parts of Devon's army were converging upon it, pouring between their parked up vehicles and from every other direction as well. Though they fired off bursts of their own as they came, some of them fell and didn't rise again.

Dragged from her seat by Annie Rae to the safety of the rear of the restaurant, Devon watched with a growing coldness halfway between frustration and fury. No matter how nice she was, the bad people simply wouldn't listen. No matter how hard she tried, they simply wouldn't learn. As Bill called her army toward the restaurant, motioning for them to get inside, she looked toward the panel van inside which Auntie still sat. Cold in answer to Devon's coldness, she ought to have been out there making people disappear by now. Perhaps she wasn't because she couldn't see what was happening outside. Fixing that right now, Devon whispered, "Auntie. Come to me."

The back of the panel van exploded, Auntie bursting through it like a birthday surprise. Behind her on both sides were the bad people. They'd come through the parked vehicles to where they had a clear sight of the front of the restaurant. Instead of firing on her, though, they scurried backward, their places taken by other bad people. They had guns of a kind Devon hadn't seen before. They opened fire, covering Auntie in splotches all of a different color, but she walked forward, ignoring them. Devon walked forward also, coming to stand beside Bill and H.

H said, "What the hell? That's paint, isn't it? Why in hell are they paintballing Auntie?"

After a long moment, Bill replied, "Solar power. They think she's solar-powered. They're trying to cut off her power supply."

"Solar-powered! How can she be solar-powered? I mean, she still works at night, doesn't she?"

"Well, I don't know. Maybe she's got reserve batteries or something. What does it matter? The fact is they're trying to give her a paint job, and we gotta stop 'em. All of you at the front get down and open up on those guys. The rest of you find towels, rags, anything. As soon as Auntie gets here, you start cleaning that paint off her. Come on, people. Move!"

All but H did. Continuing to watch Auntie, he started talking almost to himself. "Man, I wish I'd sat in on that discussion. You wanna do what? You wanna take that thing out with paintball guns? Whaddaya wanna do next? Take out an elephant with a BB gun?"

Meanwhile, windows were being smashed out all along the restaurant frontage. People knelt at their sills and fired off bursts at the paintballers. Some of them made out like they'd been hit and were dragged away as the rest began to withdraw, but not before they'd fired some parting shots at Auntie. She was now halfway to the restaurant, with large areas of her silver skin painted red, blue, yellow, and green. She didn't even notice, but then the paint barely stuck to her. It ran down her legs in rivulets, leaving a multicolored trail behind her, like the silvery path left by a slug.

Feeling like she was taking forever, Devon didn't want to wait for her to arrive. She climbed up on a sill, meaning to go meet her, but Annie Rae quickly pulled her back. "No, Devon. It's way too dangerous to go out there. You might get shot."

"No I won't. Auntie won't let them."

"Only if she can. Maybe, what with all that paint she's covered in, she might not be able to. Just wait, okay? Just let us clean her down, and then she'll be as good as new."

That could be true. Auntie certainly wasn't blowing things up and making people disappear like she usually would. Okay then. Devon would wait, but only until Auntie had been cleaned. Then she would teach these bad people a lesson, whether Annie Rae liked it or not. God had destroyed those two towns because they were full of bad people. Now Devon would destroy this one, and all the bad people would be really, really sorry for shooting her people and trying to shut Auntie down.

At last, Auntie climbed over a sill. Immediately, people with towels and clothes began to wipe her down. The paint was quickly removed, leaving not a smear behind. Auntie gleamed perfectly again. Devon looked up at her, all bright and shiny and good as new. Satisfied that she was unharmed, Devon pointed out to the parking lot and beyond. "Destroy everything."

Before anyone could object, Auntie was back out in the parking lot with Devon following close behind. She fired off a blue ball and one of Bill's panel vans screwed up on itself like an old, discarded drinks carton.

"No, silly. Not our vehicles. I meant all the bad people and their town. Come on; this way."

Taking her by the hand, Devon led her out of the parking lot and onto the highway, turning right toward the center of Kearney. All the bad people had disappeared. They must've run away, for all the good that was going to do them. Her own army followed on behind, watching with a mixture of concern and awe as Auntie destroyed building after building to either side of them, with clouds of debris scattering and clattering all around. No one attempted to stop her, not even Annie Rae, but then they shouldn't.

Auntie was obeying her queen, and so should all the rest of them.

Suddenly, the sky filled with a brilliant burst of light, and everyone except Devon fell down as if they were dead. Auntie stopped dead too. Devon tugged at her hand. "Come on. Come on; this way." But no matter how hard she tried, Auntie refused to move.

As strange as this was, it was not nearly as strange as what happened next. Right about where Auntie's forehead would have been if she had a face, a spot of brilliant white light began to glow. Out of it streamed a host of beams, light and dark and all sorts of colors as well, all of them mixed in together as if someone was shining a light through a kaleidoscope. Devon marveled at it, not thinking to look at where all that light was going until a voice behind her said, "Devon."

A man stood a few feet away, except he was like no other person she'd ever seen. He was translucent and faintly glowing, ghostly as if he wasn't really there at all. His dress was rather ordinary, a dark suit and tie, but his manner demanded attention. He might've been a school principle, with everyone knowing to be quiet and listen as soon as he walked into the room. As Devon looked upon him now, she saw an old face, much older than hers, with eyes beneath a mop of silvery hair that looked down upon her as if he could read her very thoughts.

Awestruck, suddenly she felt very small. "Are you God?"

"No. I'm the president, but I do have some very powerful new friends, very powerful. They're the ones who made it possible for me to come here like this and talk to you." His voice was deep and verging on slowness, almost like a great river meandering through a valley but always sure of its course to the sea. "It's really great that we can talk at last. I've been looking forward to it for such a long time, such a long time. I've heard all about how you want to make the world a nicer place. That's a wonderful thing to want to do, truly wonderful. We should talk about that so we can figure it out and do what's right for our country. That's what you want too, isn't it, to do what's right for our country?"

"Yes. And everywhere else as well. I want the whole world to start being nice to each other because that's what God wants too."

"Well, God is wise, a very wise person. He helped to make our country great. Did you know that? We're one nation under God, and he looks after us all. Do you know what inalienable rights are, Devon? They're the rights God gave us, and no one can take them away from us, no one can take them away. Do you know what those rights are, Devon? They're our right to do anything we want so long as we don't do anything bad. But there are bad people out there, very bad people. They don't want us to have any rights at all. They don't want us to have any rights or any fun or be able to do anything they don't like. They just want to tell everyone what to do so that everyone will be just as sad and angry as they are. But you already know that, don't you? I know you already know because you've spoken of it many times. Many, many times I've watched you speak of it."

"You've watched me? How? Was it with more drones, even after Auntie destroyed the first one?"

"No, it wasn't with more drones. Drones cost an awful lot of money, Devon, an awful lot of money. It was Auntie who watched you. She watched everything you've done, and her creators let us watch the recordings. Wonderful things you've done, Devon, wonderful things, like bringing all those people together to help you make the world a nicer place. But there are also many not-so-good things you've done, like making people disappear. Not so good. You remember those inalienable rights, the rights we all have because God gave them to us? Well, even bad people have those rights, even bad people, because that's the way God wants it. You do want to help God, don't you Devon? You do want everyone to have their inalienable rights just like God does, instead of helping the bad people try to take those rights away?"

"Yes." Devon paused. She was becoming confused again, just like Ali used to make her feel. "But if God doesn't want the bad people to be punished, why did he give Auntie to me?"

"Well, maybe God didn't give Auntie to you. Did you ever think about that? I know Ali and Ross and Tyler did. Maybe Auntie came from somewhere else, and it was all a big accident. And then she made your parents disappear, and you set out on that wonderful, wonderful journey, and you met all those people along the way. Those people told you many things, many, many things, and maybe they believed those things were true. But what if the people who told you those things didn't really know themselves? What if some of those people only told you what they wanted you to believe, so you'd do what they wanted you to do? What if some of those people were really the bad people, and they were only trying to mislead you? Did you ever think about that, Devon?"

She had thought about it many times, like with Brandon and Ali always fighting over her and James saying something very similar to Annie Rae, and all of them telling her not to trust Will. That was just grown-ups, though, always telling kids what to do. None of them had ever done anything bad that she'd seen, except maybe for Brandon wanting Auntie for himself. He might very well be a bad person, but then everyone ended up ignoring him anyway, so that was okay. As for the rest, like the elven folk around the forest fire, they'd been the ones who told her who the really bad people were, like this president, who was beginning to sound an awful lot like he wanted Auntie for himself too, just as Melissa and the bad god CIA had done.

"I don't believe you. Why would God want me to help him make the world a nicer place and then send only bad people to help me? And why wouldn't God want the bad people punished even if they do have in … inalienable rights? If God gave them those rights, then God must've decided it was okay to take them away because bad people don't deserve them. Bad people deserve to be punished and that's all."

"No, Devon. Bad people deserve to be judged, just as one day God will judge us all, including you. All those people you made disappear, so many people. Were they really bad, like your parents, or those hunters in the forest, or even Ali? Ali was a nice person, wasn't she? A good person. She looked after you like none of the others did. But you made her disappear because you were mad at her. Do you think God wanted you to do that, Devon? Do you think—"

"No! No! You're lying. You want Auntie for yourself because you're the bad person. They told me all about how you lie and steal from people. Well, you can't have her. God gave Auntie to me."

"No, Devon, I don't. Auntie doesn't belong to me. She doesn't belong to you either. She has her own creators and they want her back. Auntie must—"

"No! Auntie is mine. You're not God. You're probably not even the president, not the real one. You're just pretending so you can take her away. Well, you can't have her. She's not yours at all. She's mine."

"But Auntie is your friend, isn't she? She's your very best friend, and even very best friends have to go home when visiting is over. Well, Auntie must go home too. She has her own mommies and daddies and they're very worried about her, very worried. You don't want them to be worried about her, do you? All your friends must go home too because they have mommies and daddies who are worried about them. You must go home as well, except your mommy and daddy are no longer here to look after you. Well, that's okay. We'll look after you from now on. We'll take you somewhere safe where lots of nice people are already waiting to meet you, very nice people. They all want to be your friends, and there'll be lots of all the things you like, like ice cream, as much ice cream as you could ever want. You can have a puppy too, if you want. Wouldn't you like that, Devon, a nice, cuddly puppy to play with?"

"No! I don't want a puppy. I want Auntie."

"Auntie must go home, Devon. Everyone must go home. So be good. Be nice. Be a big, grown-up little girl and say goodbye to Auntie. Some nice people will be along to collect you very soon."

"No! No!"

But the president was gone, winking out as if someone had flicked a switch. At the same time, Devon became aware of a prickly feeling, like a balloon making her hair stand on end. Curtains of shimmering white light bathed Auntie and slowly grew more opaque. Devon knew Auntie was being taken away from her.

She took a step forward, crying. "No. Don't go. Stay here with me."

She thought it as well, but she couldn't feel Auntie anymore. There was no more warmth or cold. There was just nothing. Auntie was as unreadable to her as she'd always been to everyone else. Devon thought harder, reaching out with her hand as well as her mind. "No. Stay here with me. Please, Auntie, don't go."

Auntie didn't hear. Auntie didn't care. Quickly, the curtains of light engulfed her entirely. And then, as if she'd never been anything more than a sprinkling of glittery dust, she was gone, leaving Devon to stand all alone in the middle of her sleeping army. Looking up at the sky, she cried, "I'm sorry. I only wanted to make the world a nicer place. I didn't mean to hurt anyone. Please don't take her away. Please."

No one heard. No one answered.

"Please, Auntie, please come back. I'm sorry. You can't just go away. You can't just leave me. Take me with you. Please, Auntie, take me with you."

Eventually, with nothing more she could think of to say, all Devon could do was wail at the sky.

A NOTE FROM THE AUTHOR

If you enjoyed this book, I would be very grateful if you could write a review and publish it at your point of purchase. Your review, even a brief one, will help other readers to decide if they'll enjoy my work.

If you want to be notified of new releases from myself and other AIA Publishing authors, please sign up to the AIA Publishing email list. You'll find the sign-up button on the right-hand side under the photo at www.aiapublishing.com. Of course, your information will never be shared, and the publisher won't inundate you with emails, just let you know of new releases.

ABOUT THE AUTHOR

Remi DeWitt was born in Southampton in 1954. Adopted into an agriculture family, he left the farm to work in both the brewing industry and civil engineering, completing a degree in Physics along the way. He has since returned to the countryside and now takes long walks in between writing.

Lightning Source UK Ltd.
Milton Keynes UK
UKHW040641120722
405737UK00001B/76